"Whoever said crime doesn't pay has never spoken to Ovid Demaris."
—*New York Times*

"I certainly recommend the novels, especially the ones from Gold Medal."
—Bill Crider, *Pop Culture Magazine*

"Urgent tempo, intricate counterplotting and startling economy recalling William Ard's writing at his best."
—Anthony Boucher, *NY Times*

"Not on the bandwagon of those who glorify mobsters."
—*Amazon.com*

THE HOODS TAKE OVER

Ovid Demaris

Black Gat Books • Eureka California

THE HOODS TAKE OVER

Published by Black Gat Books
A division of Stark House Press
1315 H Street
Eureka, CA 95501, USA
griffinskye3@sbcglobal.net
www.starkhousepress.com

ISBN-13: 978-1-944520-73-1

Book design by Mark Shepard, SHEPGRAPHICS.COM
Proofreading by Bill Kelly

First Stark House Press/Black Gat Edition: April 2019

1.

The trembling finally penetrated his sleep. He fought against it at first, his sleep-soaked mind annoyed at the intrusion. Then he was wide awake, sitting up in the double bed, looking down at Edie, his hand groping in the darkness for the lamp switch above the headboard.

She lay big in the bed, her once thin waist now bloated by nine months of pregnancy. The sudden glare of light startled her and she quickly flipped over on her side, away from him, burying her tear-stained face in the pillow.

"Please, Alan," she whispered in a trembling voice, "don't look at me." And she began to moan, slowly rocking her heavy body, her long, shapely fingers fiercely gripping the pillow.

"Migraine?" he asked, feeling foolish in his helplessness.

"Yes. I think I'm going crazy." She turned to look at him, her body still rocking with the pain.

He reached over and gently brushed her dark brown hair from her perspiring face. Her forehead was cold and clammy. "You need an injection," he said. "I'll fix it."

"Don't," she groaned, suddenly sitting up in the bed. Then she was in his arms, her face pressed against his chest; and he held her trembling body in silence for a long time.

"I want the baby. I really do," she whispered fiercely. "You believe that, don't you?"

"Of course."

"I want it more than anything else on earth. We've waited twelve years, and now it's here ... and I'm happy. Truly happy. You've got to believe that. You've got to." The sobs tore at her throat, strangling her.

"I've never doubted it," he said, holding her tightly, suddenly beginning to doubt.

She pushed away from him and flipped her hair back with a wild toss of her head. She waited before speaking, struggling for control.

"The doctor said migraine was quite common during pregnancy ..." She hesitated, slowly turning her eyes away to avoid his.

"Well, then," he said, "that explains it. Now let me get the injection. You must have some sleep."

"It doesn't explain it," she cried, suddenly frantic. "You don't understand. It's subconscious."

"What?"

"It's subconscious. Don't you understand?"

"No. I don't."

"Oh, please," she cried, helplessly, throwing herself into his arms, her fingernails biting into his back. "I want the baby. I do, I do, I do."

"Of course you do."

"But I'm afraid. I felt it move again tonight. The time is getting nearer, and I'm ... I'm ... I'm afraid, Alan. So afraid."

He patted her head reassuringly. "Poor baby," he said, "don't be afraid. There's really nothing to be afraid of."

"I'm too small. I know it. Something dreadful will happen."

"Nothing will happen. Everything will be all right. I promise you."

"Oh, Alan! I'm so ashamed. It's the migraine. It drives me insane. It feels as if the whole side of my head is coming off."

"Now, look, just relax and I'll fix you an injection. It'll take just a minute."

"No, Alan. I'm out of D.H.E.," she murmured. And the trembling started again. "But please don't worry. I'll be all right in a little while." She pushed out of his arms and sank back onto the bed.

He looked down at her sadly. Her stomach was so big and the rest of her was so small, he wanted to cry. "Look, it won't take me a minute to run down and get the prescription refilled. There's an all-night drugstore on Hollywood Boulevard."

"I don't want you to leave me. I'm afraid something will happen. I think I'm ready."

"Are you getting labor pains?"

"No, but there's a lot of movement and my back aches way down here," and she moved her hand down to the small of her back.

"Honey, it's only about a mile away. I can run down there and be back in fifteen minutes. Nothing can possibly happen in that time." He stood up and began dressing.

She turned on her side and watched him, her eyes wide with the pain. "What has happened to me?" she asked.

"Nothing," he said, slipping into his trousers. "You're just going through a tough period."

"I'm becoming a neurotic."

"No, you're not. Now just relax and I'll be right back. If the headache gets worse, why don't you get up and have some coffee. Might do you some good." He finished buttoning the sport shirt and moved over to the bed. She tried to smile when he kissed her forehead.

"Don't run," she said, as he hurried across the room. "There's no emergency."

"I'll take a cab back if I can find one," he said. "And you take it easy."

It was one o'clock in the morning when he arrived at the all-night drugstore. He waited while the short, heavyset pharmacist examined the prescription through thick-lensed spectacles, then looked up and smiled a professional and knowing smile.

"Is this for yourself?"

"No. My wife."

"Migraine can be a terrible burden on a person. My mother had migraine for twenty years. Needed a great deal of care and attention. Sometimes it would just about drive her out of her mind. Very bad, indeed." And he shook his head and pursed his lips.

"Could you hurry, please?" Alan asked. He was having trouble with his breathing. He felt weak and dizzy after the mile-long run.

"Has your wife tried Emperin Compound Number Three?"

"No."

"How about Cafergot? Very good, you know. That's what my mother took. This D.H.E. 45 never did her any good."

"Please hurry," Alan said, more sharply this time. He leaned against the counter for support.

The pharmacist's magnified eyes stared at him for a moment. "Are you all right?"

"Yes," Alan said. "But please hurry with the prescription."

Suddenly, time seemed vitally important to him. He had to get back home. Something was happening inside of him that he could not quite understand. But if he were going to be sick, he wanted to be home when it happened.

He watched the pharmacist move slowly to a cabinet. "Do you want six or twelve ampules?"

"Twelve, please."

The pharmacist came back to the counter. He took a label from a glass container and carefully placed it into the typewriter. Slowly, methodically, using only one finger, he typed out the instructions. Then he raised the label to his mouth and his tongue flicked across it. He looked up and smiled.

"Tastes like cherry," he said. "It's a big improvement from that old mucilage taste." He held on to the package, smiling at Alan.

"How much is it?"

"You know, you ought to consider Cafergot. Have your wife ask her doctor about it. It's a lot easier to take. It's a tablet. All you need is a little water. This D.H.E. is a nuisance. You know, injection and all. Cafergot will go to work just as fast, too. Maybe even a little faster. Have your wife ask her doctor."

"I will," Alan said, fighting against the dizziness sweeping over him.

"You won't be sorry."

"I promise," Alan said. "Now, please, how much do I owe you?"

"Oh, let me see, now. I've got the price list here somewhere. Not much call for this stuff, you know. Now, Cafergot, I could tell you the price just like that." He snapped his fingers.

"Please," Alan said. "Can't you understand? I'm in a hurry!"

"Won't take a second. I got the list here someplace. Oh, here it is. Twelve one-cc ampules ... that's eight dollars and fifty cents ... plus tax, of course. Now, let me see, that's four per cent tax. Four times eight, that's thirty-two, plus two, that's thirty-four cents, plus eight-fifty ... that's eight dollars and eighty-four cents."

By this time Alan could barely focus on him. He dropped a five and four ones on the counter and snatched the package out of the startled pharmacist's hands.

"Wait! You've got change coming," he called, but Alan did not hear him.

He was already running down Hollywood Boulevard.

At one o'clock in the morning, Hollywood Boulevard is as dead as Forest Lawn Cemetery. It's like any other small town. The sidewalks are rolled up at midnight and everyone either goes home to bed or somewhere else for kicks. Cabbies had long ago abandoned the area for lusher territory like the Sunset Strip. This Friday morning was no exception.

Alan did not stop running until he reached the corner of Sycamore Avenue. A sleek Jaguar raced by, gunning its motor, the roar echoing down the deserted street. Alan tried to watch the sports car speeding down the boulevard. It became extremely important to him. If only he could focus on the red taillights, clear his vision, then maybe he would be all right. He stood on the sidewalk, his tall, thin body leaning forward, his eyes narrowed to slits, desperately trying to focus on the disappearing spots of red. But the more he concentrated on them, the more blurred they became.

Then the Jag was gone and he felt cheated. It was then that the real pain hit him.

It arrived full force.

It felt as though a small bomb had exploded in his chest.

This was a strange pain, something he had never before experienced. He knew he had to get off the street and he started walking up Sycamore Avenue. Suddenly, he felt very calm. It was as though he had expected it. And he knew exactly where the pain was and how large it was. His hand went to his chest and he pressed against the pain, trying to relieve it, but it was no good. Somehow the dizziness had gone and there was only the pain, hot and piercing. He stopped near the entrance to a parking lot and took a deep breath. It was not so bad after all.

Then a second bomb exploded, right next to the first one, and he felt himself go limp.

He staggered into the parking lot, away from the street

lights, and sat down in the heavy darkness.

A third bomb exploded.

All three explosions merged into one burning, searing pain moving across his chest. It was difficult for him to breathe, and he struggled against the pain, hoping that it would soon disappear.

But the next thing he knew, his left arm had become numb, and he pinched it, trying to stimulate the circulation. For a fleeting moment, he was afraid to die. The awareness of death swept over him, and he saw a vision of himself dead. Embalmed. Lying stiff, like a wax statue, in a coffin. And he saw Edie leaning over his coffin, weeping.

The thought sent stark terror shooting through him. He fought against it, against death itself. He was too young to die: thirty-five.

That was not even middle age. He was so young and had so much to live for. Edie and the child. The child they had tried for twelve years to conceive.

Then he remembered Edie's migraine and he tried to get up. But it was no use. No use at all. He sat in the darkness and waited for the pain to release him.

They waited in the black Cadillac just a hundred feet away from Alan Avery. Two men patiently waiting to commit murder. The murder of Slick Danchik.

Joe Ricca grunted and shifted his two hundred pounds slightly to give himself a better view of the parking lot.

"For Christ sakes, Axe, shut up. You're getting on my goddam nerves."

Abe (the Axe) Doto glanced at Joe without moving his large head. He resented being talked to in that way, but he was smart enough to conceal it.

"What the hell," he whined, and he hated himself for sounding like that. "We've been sitting here for over an hour. What if the bastard don't show?"

"He'll show."

"He could stay all night."

"Marsha knows better than to let him stay all night."

"Yeah, well, I don't know. That Slick is hot for them whores."

"That son of a bitch better get good and laid cause it's his last time."

"Yeah," Axe laughed. "He's gonna die a satisfied man. Christ, am I gonna enjoy giving it to that bastard. The lousy fink."

"Don't get ahead of yourself," Ricca warned. "When the time comes to give it to him, I'm the guy that's gonna do the giving. I'm gonna cut his goddamn throat for him. Understand? No son of a bitch puts the heat on me and lives. No Slick Danchik or Abe Doto or nobody. And don't you ever forget it."

"For Christ sakes, Joe; don't talk like that. I'm no fink."

"I'm just telling you. That's all. Take it for what it's worth. No son-of-a-bitching bastard puts the heat on me and lives. I'm gonna cut his goddam heart out, hear me?"

"Jesus, Joe. You and me been together a long time. Hell, we been together since the thirties in Brooklyn. Christ, Joe, you're like a brother to me. Like a goddam brother. I mean it, Joe."

"So you mean it. But just remember what I said. This goddam bit tonight is something you better forget but quick."

"What's the matter with you, Joe? You've never talked to me like that before. I tell you, Joe. You're like a brother to me. So please, God damn it, don't talk like that to me." He didn't mind the whine now. He couldn't even hear it.

"Don't get excited."

"Don't get excited, he says," Axe looked around as if addressing an audience. "Christ, who wouldn't get excited.”

"Keep your goddam voice down. And remember. I don't want nothing to happen here. We take him out to that spot in the desert. That way we just drop him in the hole and fill it up. Understand?"

"Sure, sure. But what if he gives us trouble?"

"He won't give us no trouble."

"Where is the bastard?"

"Relax. Here, have a butt. We got all night."

2.

Slick Danchik really was a hot man with the whores. And he liked to keep things running smooth and slick. You got the urge, you took care of it. No problems. No complications. And no goddam wedding bells. Man, that was the worst drag of all. He stood before the dresser mirror, adjusting his hand-painted silk tie, thinking about the little redhead that had just left. Well, maybe, she wasn't a real redhead. Hell, he hadn't had time to really check. What was the difference, anyway. She was a real cute little number. Plenty of everything, too. And what was more important, she knew what to do with it. Every bit of it. Hell, he'd have to see her again. Her name was Kitty. That was cute. Fitted her to a "t." A double "t." He laughed at that. Maybe he ought to call her back. Why wait for later when you can do it right now.

He crossed the room and opened the door. "Hey, Kitty!" he called down the empty hall. "Come back here."

A door opened and Slick saw Marsha Brown's head peer out.

"Go home," she said.

"I wanta go another round."

"Kitty's gone. Come back tomorrow." And the head

disappeared behind the closed door. Marsha Brown ran the houses in Los Angeles for the Kahn-Ricca combine. She was a tall, thin woman who looked more like a *Vogue* model than the boss of a flesh shop.

Slick went back into the room and finished dressing. The last thing on his mind at this moment was Joe Ricca. It was true that he had agreed to turn state's evidence in the narcotics case involving Ricca and half a dozen other hoods, but that was a secret between Slick and the police. Ricca couldn't possibly know about it. He'd find out soon enough, though, when the trial started. But by then it would be too late. Ricca was good for at least ten years. That's what Slick would have gotten if he hadn't cooperated. Ten years. That was a long time between lays. Longer than Slick wanted to think about.

He slipped into the gray shetland jacket and studied his reflection in the mirror. Not bad. Not bad at all. He took out his comb and carefully passed it through his black curly hair. It was getting a little too long. It looked good, though. The way the ends curled. Maybe he would let it grow a little longer. Just get it trimmed around the sides. He put the comb away into his inside jacket pocket, and peered closely into the mirror. He brushed his eyebrows back with his fingertips and slowly winked at himself in the mirror. Then he laughed. Goddam. What a riot! Man, he could really go at times.

He went out into the long hallway and took the back stairs. It was dark out in the alley and for a moment he felt uneasy. What the hell, he thought. I've got nothing to worry about. Nevertheless, he quickened his step until he reached the sidewalk and the security of a street lamp. He stopped, looked up and down the empty street, forced himself to take out a cigarette casually and light it. His hand trembled a little. Jesus H. Christ, he thought. What's happening to me? Next thing I'm going to start whistling and then I'll be walking up the middle of the street.

He started walking again, more slowly this time, the cigarette held between lipstick-smeared lips, his hands casually stuck into his trouser pockets.

Slick Danchik stood fifty feet away from death.

When Ricca first saw the red glow of the cigarette his hands began to perspire. He watched Slick walk into the parking lot and each step did something to his insides. It was like the beating of a drum. He could feel the excitement mounting inside. Keeping his eyes on Danchik, he nudged Doto with his elbow and they stepped out of the car and waited there in the darkness.

Slick stopped ten feet away from them and felt in his jacket pockets for the car keys. He coughed and sparks flew from the cigarette. A wisp of smoke drifted into his eye and he cursed, rubbing at the smarting eye with the back of his hand. When he took his hand away, Ricca and Doto were standing before him.

"I don't want a goddam word out of you, Slick," Ricca said, his fingers digging into Slick's thin biceps.

"Hey, what gives?" Slick asked, looking from Ricca to Doto.

Ricca's fist pounded into Slick's stomach. The cigarette flew out of his mouth. His knees buckled and he began to cough, tears running down his cheeks.

"Not one goddam word," Ricca said.

"Please, Joe," Slick managed to say between coughs. "Let me ..."

The fist pounded in again, harder this time, and Slick sagged forward. Axe caught him around the head and lifted him up straight.

"Christ, Joe," Slick whispered. "Give me a ..."

"You son of a bitch," Ricca cursed, and this time his fist caught Slick on the side of the jaw. Blood spurted out of his open mouth and he began to whimper.

Ricca caught him by the coat lapels and brought Slick's face up to his.

"Listen, you little fink," he spat the words into the bleeding face. "No bastard puts the heat on Joe Ricca and lives. You're dead." And he gave him a violent push.

Slick staggered back on his heels, struggling for balance, his arms waving wildly. Then he was running, running for his life. Running straight for the wall of the building on the east side of the parking lot. He hit the wall and bounced off. He spun around and saw Ricca and Doto coming toward him. Ricca held a knife in the palm of his hand.

"Axe, get on the other side," Ricca commanded. And the two men spread out, slowly moving forward, sealing all ways of escape.

Alan Avery sat in the darkness, his back leaning against the brick wall of the building on the south side of the parking lot. He waited for the burning pain in the center of his chest to subside. At first he was aware of the passing of time, then he lost track of it. The only thing that was real and important was the pain. It became an entity, a part of him, like the growth of another organ. Except this was the only organ. There was nothing else. Only the pain and the mind that felt that pain. And the two had become one.

It was then that he saw the man running and the two men following him. The man ran right past him, and he heard him crying. Then the man hit the wall, and Alan heard the dull thud of the head striking the hard brick. He saw the two men slowly approaching the cornered man. The man was sobbing wildly now, beyond control, and Alan wanted to rush to his aid, but he couldn't even move. It was all he could do to breathe. He watched, hypnotized by the stark violence, his legs trembling with fear and horror.

They were closing in quickly now, and Slick panicked. There was a car parked in front of him and for a moment it looked as if he was going to crawl under it. Then suddenly he leaped forward, like a diver doing a swan from the high board, and landed on top of the hood, his head striking hard against the windshield. Then he was crawling and slipping, his feet kicking wildly, his fingers helpless against the hard polished metal.

Ricca and Doto ran up, but before they could reach him, Slick was standing on top of the car, looking around wildly, his hands holding his head. Then he realized there was no place else to go and he just stood there whimpering.

Ricca and Doto stood by the car, looking up at him. "You're dead, you fink," Ricca said.

"Please, Joe," he sobbed. "Don't. Please!"

Just then the Axe grabbed him by an ankle. Slick yelled in surprise and tried to kick. The Axe gave a hard yank and Slick spun around in mid-air and landed on his back, his head leaning over the other side of the car, right into Ricca's arms. Ricca's fist closed over Slick's long curly hair and for a second the two men gazed into each other's eyes. Then the knife made one long, quick stroke and Slick's throat burst open. Ricca stepped back as the blood spurted out, black and warm and sticky.

"Axe, get the Cad," Ricca said, as Doto came around from the other side of the car. "Let's get this bastard buried."

It was two o'clock when the black-and-white radio patrol car swung left off Vine and slowly headed west on Hollywood Boulevard. This was the fourth time around for Sergeant Ernie Tucker and Patrolman Bob Cross, and so far nothing had happened. Nothing, that is, except a couple of minor traffic accidents, and, of course, the hysterical blonde in the white Lincoln Continental.

"That was Sally Paige," Cross said, the awe still in his voice.

"Who's Sally Paige?" Tucker grunted, scooting down in the seat, his knees resting on the dashboard.

"The movie star," Cross replied, surprised at Tucker's ignorance. "Christ, everybody knows Sally Paige."

"Yeah. Well, I don't. And besides, movie star or no movie star, she was drunk and should have been booked."

"Hell she was. She might have had a couple of drinks, but she wasn't drunk. Christ, that would have been a hell of a thing to do. She's just a kid."

"Nuts. She's old enough to drink, she's old enough to book."

Cross ignored the remark. "Did you see that character she hit? Christ, a real vulture. He would have sued the bejesus out of her if we had booked her for drunken driving."

"Listen, kid. How old are you?"

Cross gave Tucker a suspicious glance. "Twenty-four."

"Been to college?"

"Stanford."

"Played football?"

"Right end. Three years on the varsity."

"And now you've just finished police school. Right?"

"Well, eight months ago."

"Tell me something, will you? Why does a young, clean-cut, educated fellow like yourself have to cuss and swear with every word? What's the reason? Are you trying to appear tough? Is that what it is?"

"Hell, I don't know," Cross mumbled. "It just comes out."

"Look, kid. I'm forty years old and I weigh about one-eighty-five and stand five-eleven in my stocking feet.

You've got at least thirty pounds on me and a good two inches, plus sixteen years. But don't confuse yourself about who's tough and who ain't. I've been batting around this police force for nineteen years and there ain't a hood in this town who has any doubt about whether I'm tough. And I never had to swear to prove it."

Bob Cross saw the light turn amber and brought the patrol car to a slow stop. He could feel the blood rushing up his neck and face, and he didn't dare trust his voice. So he just sat there, without speaking, his eyes staring fixedly ahead. Who in hell did that old bastard think he was talking to anyway? What gave him the right to talk like that? Nineteen years on the force and he was back riding a patrol car with a rookie. Big deal. Yet, Cross had no doubt how tough Tucker was. All he had to do was look at him. That was all. Just take one good look into those dark, deep-set eyes and you knew, all right.

Tucker realized that Cross was angry, and for a moment he was sorry he had spouted off at the kid. Not too sorry, though. Not sorry enough to apologize. And, anyway, someone had to straighten him out. A good-looking kid like that didn't have to go around swearing to prove any-thing. He was big enough to back up a clear simple sen-tence without the help of swear words.

Tucker was a cop with a mission. His burning hatred of all criminals had become the central motivating force in his life. Everything else had become secondary, unimpor-tant. He had never married and hadn't been out on a date in ten years. He slept in a small one-room kitchenette apartment in an old substandard apartment building on Western Avenue, just south of Melrose. He lived all over the city. He was on duty twenty-four hours a day, seven days a week. He was always the cop. Always looking for trouble. And he always knew where to find it.

On six occasions, in the performance of his duty—although four of the times he was officially off duty—Tucker had used his service revolver to kill. Each time the newspapers had played it up and he had gone up before the police board, and each time he had been fully exonerated.

Only a few of the oldtimers on the force knew the real story behind Tucker's dedication. And of those, none had ever had the courage to discuss it in his presence....

The story began when Tucker was only eighteen. The same month he made All-State quarterback. He was a senior at Los Angeles High School, taking a college preparatory course, and had half a dozen football scholarships in his pocket. The future looked bright. His father, Ben Tucker, a lieutenant on the vice squad, had been both father and mother to him since the death of his mother when he was fourteen. He loved and admired his father. Every summer they went on trips together. One summer when he was sixteen his father took him to Europe.

They spent two months touring France, Germany, Austria, Italy and England. Ernie never forgot that trip and he never forgot how kind his father had been to him. What a swell team they had made.

One night they even went out on a date together. They picked up a couple of young girls and went out on the town. Really painted it red. What a night it had been. The memory of it returned to him often through the years. And when it did, he could actually see his father, sitting at the table with the two girls, laughing at some American joke he was trying to translate into French. Why, he could even hear the laughter, deep and rich and loud.

Then one night, two years later, his father came home and a sawed-off shotgun went off, taking off half of his head. Ernie heard the shot and when he found his father, he was already dead. Two weeks later they found the killer and everything went crazy. The newspapers flashed the news that Ben Tucker had been a crooked cop, his killing the result of a doublecross.

Ernie left school and joined the Navy. But before leaving he visited everyone from the Vice Squad Captain to the Police Commissioner, and pleaded for his father's name to be cleared. But everywhere it was the same. They shook their heads sadly and spoke the same words. Ben Tucker had been a crooked cop. Period.

Bob Cross was the first to see Alan Avery. He was standing in the middle of Hollywood Boulevard, waving at the approaching patrol car.

"What the hell," Cross said, glancing at Tucker.

Tucker slowly raised his head without answering. He was still in Paris, reliving a scene from their trip up the Eiffel Tower. They were having lunch and his father was expounding on the beauty of Paris. And then he laughed, a little embarrassed, and said that the city was almost as beautiful as its women. "How would you like a little Frenchie for a mother?" he had asked, now even more embarrassed. And Ernie had laughed timidly and said, "Fine. I'll be the envy of the football squad."

Cross slammed on the brakes. Tucker looked up and saw Alan Avery standing in front of the car. He looked drunk. Sloppy drunk.

"Well," Cross said as he stepped out of the car. "The night wouldn't be complete without a drunk. I'll take care of him, Sergeant."

Sergeant, is it, Tucker thought, and smiled. Go ahead and be a prima donna. Maybe it will make you feel better. He watched Cross approach the tall, thin man and talk to him. They were standing in front of the patrol car and the man leaned against it for support. Tucker took out a cigarette and lighted it. He inhaled deeply, keeping his eyes on the two men. The man was talking rapidly and he seemed to have difficulty breathing. Then he pulled out his wallet and slowly went through his identification papers.

"Please," Alan said, "can't you understand? A man was just murdered in the parking lot on Sycamore." And he stopped to take another deep breath. It seemed he couldn't get enough air into his lungs.

Cross took out his report book and started to write. "Your name is Alan Avery. Right?"

"Yes," Alan said. And then he repeated his address while Cross wrote it down.

"Come with me," Cross said, leading Alan to the patrol car. He opened the back door and Alan stepped inside and sat down. Cross went around and got in on the driver's side. Alan saw that the other policeman was looking at him and he tried to smile.

"I've been telling this policeman that I've just witnessed a murder and he doesn't seem to believe me."

Tucker turned and looked at Cross, who shook his head.

"I don't know, Sergeant. This is Alan Avery and he claims he was in a parking lot and witnessed a murder. I can't smell any liquor on his breath but he seems rocky as hell."

Tucker turned his eyes to Alan and held out his hand. "Take out the money and hand me your wallet," he said.

"Says he's a teacher at Hollywood High School," Cross said, as Tucker examined Alan's papers under the car's dome light.

"What did you expect?" Tucker said, handing the wallet back to Alan. "Another movie star?" And he looked at Alan and smiled. "What were you doing in the parking lot, Mr. Avery?"

Alan looked down, embarrassed. "I was ill," he said, softly.

"But why the parking lot?"

"I was going by the parking lot when I became ill. I didn't want to be ill on the street, so I went into the lot and sat down for a moment, waiting for the seizure to pass."

"What kind of seizure?"

"I don't know," Alan said. "I think it was indigestion."

"What happened then?"

"A man came into the lot and two other men starting beating him up. He ran and they chased him. Then the man climbed on top of a car and fell. One of the men cut his throat with a knife. Then they loaded him in the trunk of a big Cadillac and drove off. It was the most horrifying thing I've ever seen. He just took his knife and slit the man's throat wide open. It was horrible."

"Could you describe the men?"

"I don't know," Alan said. "It was very dark."

"I see," Tucker said. "Tell Patrolman Cross how to get there."

Alan gave the directions and the police car turned north on Sycamore and stopped before the parking lot.

"Drive inside," Tucker said. "Right up to where the guy was killed."

Alan directed them right to the spot and all three men got out. Tucker and Cross played flashlights on the ground until they found the blood. Tucker squatted down and rubbed a finger in the puddle of blood.

"It's still fairly warm," he said, standing up.

"My God," Cross said, staring down at all the blood. "They really drained him."

"Okay," Tucker said, turning to Alan. "Let's go over this again. And you, Bob, write it down. Describe the killers as well as you can. You know, height, weight, complexion; anything you can tell up will help."

"One was tall and stocky. I'd say about six feet and maybe over two hundred pounds. The other was quite short and very fat. He seemed to have a large head. I remember he couldn't run fast. You know, he sort of waddled. As far as I could tell, they were both of dark complexion. That's about all I can tell you."

"How about the victim?"

"He was of average height and weight. Dark complexion also. Maybe it' s because it was so dark in here and things happened so fast."

"Were they Mexicans?"

"I don't think so."

"Anything else?"

"Yes, I did get one thing I'm sure you can use."

"What's that?"

"The license number. It was YSD eight nine two oh. And the car was the latest model Cadillac. It was black and very big. The biggest model they make, I believe."

Tucker turned and playfully tapped Cross on the shoulder, laughing. "There," he said. "You can have your movie stars. I'll take a schoolteacher every time."

"It might be stolen plates," Cross said.

"Might be, but I doubt it. This looks like a quiet little job where they didn't expect trouble."

"I hope so," Cross said, doubtfully.

"Get on the radio," Tucker said. "Get headquarters to put out an all-car broadcast on a possible murder and kidnaping. Have them send homicide and the crime lab down here. Give them all the information you've got. And tell that dispatcher that I want the make on that license number as soon as D&M runs it through."

Tucker went back to the blood and played his flashlight around. Alan followed him. Tucker went down on his knees and peered under the car. The light beam moved slowly, stopping every now and then, as Tucker examined everything that was not part of the asphalt. Finally he stood up and carefully brushed his trousers.

"Nothing here," he said, smiling at Alan. For some unknown reason he felt proud of Alan. He wanted to pat him on the back, shake his hand, but he just smiled.

"I should be getting home," Alan said. "My wife is quite ill."

"Your wife is ill, too?"

"Yes, you see I came down to the drugstore to get her prescription refilled. She's pregnant and gets terrible migraine headaches. That's how I happened to be here. I ran and I think it was too much for me. I got an awful pain in my chest. It sort of paralyzed me."

"You should see a doctor," Tucker said, surprised at his concern for a stranger.

"Oh, I'll be all right," Alan said. "But I should be getting home. Edie will be awfully worried."

"Well, I don't know," Tucker said. "You should wait for the homicide boys to get down here first. They'll want to question you. And then you'll have to go downtown and make a statement before a hearing secretary."

"But couldn't I go home first and come back?"

"I'm afraid not. But, look, as soon as Lieutenant Johnson gets here we'll see what we can do. Okay?"

"Well," Alan said. "I'll wait a little longer."

Cross came running back and his voice was full of excitement when he spoke. "Jesus," he cried. "We really hit the jackpot this time. It took D&M three minutes flat to run a make on that license number. It belongs to Joe Ricca. If I'm not mistaken that's pretty big-time. Right, Sergeant?"

Tucker just stared at him. He couldn't believe it. Joe Ricca! Marty Kahn's partner. Ricca had been big in organized crime for years. His success started when he left New York to evade trial during the Murder Inc. investigation. He went to Chicago, then to Cleveland, where he met Marty Kahn. They teamed up and migrated to Los

Angeles, Marty's home town, in 1946.

In ten years they had reached the top of the heap. They had organized all of Southern California. Only recently had things started to go wrong. Ricca and five others had been arrested on a narcotics charge. Ricca was presently out on twenty-five-thousand-dollars' bail.

Marty Kahn himself was out on bail on two different charges. One for one hundred thousand dollars on conspiracy to commit assault and robbery. The other for five thousand dollars on suspicion of bookmaking.

In a career that spanned over thirty years in crime, Joe Ricca had served only six months for assault in Chicago. Back in Brownsville, he had been an intimate friend of Kid Twist and Pittsburgh Phil during the heyday of Murder Inc., and was rated among the best in the business of execution, with at least thirty murders to his credit. Now, Tucker thought, Joseph Ricca is where we want him.

"Yes," Tucker said. "It's big. Just as big as you can get in this town."

"What a break!" Cross grinned.

Alan looked at the two officers and thought of Edie. "Sergeant, I've got to get home. I can't wait any longer."

Tucker gave him a quick look and turned to Cross. "Bob, I'm gonna drive Mr. Avery home. His wife is sick. Tell Lieutenant Johnson we'll be right back. Explain it to him."

"Okay, Sergeant. Let's say I'll try to explain. With the lieutenant I'm not sure it's possible. But I'll give it the old college try."

3.

Sergeant Ernie Tucker drove Alan home in the patrol car. He waited outside while Alan went into the house. Edie was sitting drinking coffee at the kitchen table when Alan came in. She tried to smile, but Alan could see that she was in excruciating pain, and he hurried to the bathroom without explaining. He opened the medicine cabinet and took out the case with the syringe. He opened the package of ampules and took one out. It was a little glass vial, shaped to a fine point. There was a little saw attached to it and he used it to cut the tip of the ampule. Then he took out the syringe and stuck the needle into the little hole and pulled back on the plunger, draining the ampule with one pull. He held the syringe up and pressed on the plunger slightly, just enough to release any air that might be in the syringe. He watched as little bubbles formed at the tip of the needle, until the liquid was coming out clean and solid. He walked back into the kitchen, the syringe held up in front of him.

Edie got up and went into the bedroom without speaking. She stretched out on the bed, her face buried into the pillow, her arms gripping it tightly. Alan raised her nightgown and slowly stuck the needle into the muscle of her left buttock. He felt a shiver go through her as he pressed down on the plunger.

"That does it," he said, trying to be cheerful. And he gently and affectionately patted her on the other buttock as he pulled the needle out. She didn't move and he caressed her for a moment, marveling at the softness of the skin, his hand moving down into the inside of her thighs.

"Don't, please," she sighed, turning over on her back. "I look, awful."

"You look beautiful to me," he said. "You always do." And he passed his hand over the swelling of her stomach.

She pushed his hand away and reached for the covers, bringing them up to her chin. "Now I feel a little safer," she said, trying to laugh, but the pain was still with her and Alan noticed how the muscles on the left side of her face were contorting.

"It won't be long now," he said. "You'll feel fine."

He went back into the bathroom and cleaned the syringe and replaced it in the medicine cabinet. He felt better now and looked at himself in the mirror. His skin looked white and pasty, and his eyes were bloodshot. For a moment he started taking his pulse, but quickly gave it up. He had forgotten about the count. He didn't remember whether it was supposed to be sixty-eight or ninety-eight. Anyway, it wouldn't help anything. Besides, except for a minor headache, he felt normal enough. He took a couple of aspirins and went back into the bedroom.

Edie was sitting up in the bed, smiling. She held out her arms and he went to her and sat down on the bed.

"Aren't you coming to bed?" she asked. "I feel fine now. It's as if someone had actually extracted a horrible monster from my head." She held him tightly in her arms. "I love you," she whispered. "You're so good to me."

"I'm sorry I took so long," he said, pulling away from her. "There's something I must tell you."

"What is it?" she asked, her eyes worried.

"Well," he said, hesitating. "I really don't know how to tell you."

"What do you mean?" she asked, now really worried. "Did something happen?"

"I was a witness to a murder," he said, quickly, wanting to get it over with. "I saw the whole thing. Two men killed a man right before my eyes. It was a terrifying experience."

"Oh, Alan!" she said, and held him tightly. "Did they see you?"

"No," he said, "but I gave the police a good description of the men and the license number of their car."

She stared at him, horrified. "You didn't!"

"Didn't what?" he asked, surprised by her reaction.

"You didn't tell the police?"

"Why, of course I did. What else could I do? I saw the whole thing. I had no choice."

"Oh, Alan," and she was crying, holding on to him, her body trembling against his.

"Edie! What's the matter?"

"Those men will kill you."

"Now, wait a minute." He tried to laugh. "Aren't you being a little melodramatic? This is not the movies, you know. Things like that don't really happen to law-abiding citizens."

"Alan, you're so naive."

"Just a minute. I don't think I like that. I just happen to think that we're living in a civilized world. You've seen too many gangster movies."

She stopped crying and stared at him. "That's what I mean," she said. "You really believe that. You think that gangsters only exist in the movies. Was that a real murder you saw tonight?"

"Yes, it was a real murder. And, no, I don't think gangsters exist only in the movies. All I said was that law-abiding citizens are protected from gangsters. That's why we have a police force. We are in no danger. So please don't be afraid. Everything will be all right. As I told you, the police already have the name of one of the gangsters. They're going to arrest him tonight. And that's going to be the end of it."

"I hope you're right," she said. "I hope to God you're right."

"I am. Please believe that. Now I have to go. There's a policeman outside waiting for me. I have to go back to headquarters and make a statement. You go to sleep. I'll be back as soon as I can."

He leaned forward and kissed her. Her arms went around his waist and she crushed him against her swelling stomach, her soft lips demanding against his.

Sergeant Tucker waited in the patrol car. A cop gets used to waiting, and Tucker had had nineteen years to get used to it. But tonight it was different. Tonight he was anxious to get going. He wanted to be the one to pick up Ricca. That was something he'd enjoy. Something really special. Tucker knew that Ricca was responsible for his being assigned to patrol. Everybody on the force knew it.

Tucker had spent four months of his spare time gathering evidence against Marsha Brown, showing how she ran all prostitution in the city for Ricca and Kahn. Then he submitted it to his superior, Lieutenant Finch, who coldly thanked him for his extracurricular efforts, and mumbled something about checking into it as soon as possible.

One week later Tucker was transferred from the Vice Squad to the Patrol Detail. Nothing more was ever heard about the report on Marsha Brown. Finch became incommunicado as far as Tucker was concerned. Tucker knew the chain of command—and Joe Ricca was at the head of that chain. The way Tucker understood it, prostitution and narcotics were Ricca's domain in Los Angeles. Marty Kahn ran all bookmaking, gambling and extortion.

Now the story was changing. Ricca's career was coming to an end. And all because a teacher, a nice, quiet teacher was going to put the finger on Joe Ricca, and there was nothing that Finch or any other crooked cop could do about it.

Tucker took out a cigarette and lit it. He puffed and smiled vaguely at the thick, lazily curling smoke. There was an old saying about every man getting his hour in court. Now was the time for Ricca to get his. Maybe something would be done about organized crime; maybe the newspapers would scream loud enough for even the commissioner to hear. And it was ironical. Just because a teacher happened to be sick. Life was full of little ironies, but this one topped them all. A smart hood like Ricca could go on for years committing every crime in the book, flaunting the law at every turn, and never spend a day in jail, while law-abiding citizens filled the jails for negligent acts or errors in judgment. But sometimes the Riccas also made errors in judgment. Like tonight. And when they did, they also went to jail. And often to the chair, or the gas chamber, or the hangman's noose....

When Alan came out, Tucker was listening to the all-car broadcast. It had been on the air for twenty minutes now and the operator sounded slightly bored.

Tucker turned it down and smiled at Alan. "Everything all right?"

"Yes, my wife is much better."

"Fine," Tucker said. "Now we can get some work done."

Lieutenant Sam Johnson had been on the homicide detail for nearly thirty years. He was a robust man of fifty-four, with a round, red face and small, dull, almost colorless eyes that had once been very blue. Nothing ever surprised or excited Sam Johnson. He handled every kind of violence a big city could dish out with the phlegmatic air of an Englishman at tea.

Tonight was no exception. He walked around the parking lot, which was now as lighted up as a Hollywood premiere, grunted at remarks from the crime lab technicians, stopping to study anything that caught his attention.

When Tucker and Alan arrived, Sam Johnson was standing in front of the car where Danchik had been murdered. One of the fingerprint experts was explaining about the condition of the prints available.

"Everything is smeared. There are prints everywhere but not one I can use. I'll tell you. That guy did a lot of scratching before he died. Come here. Look at the paint on this hood. It looks as if a fan hit it. There's blood on the windshield. There's blood and plenty of skin on that brick wall over there. But there's not a damn print I can use anywhere. This guy was moving too fast."

Sam Johnson listened, nodding his head at times, his small eyes studying everything.

"Okay, Lester," he said. "You keep on looking. Maybe you'll run into something."

"I doubt it, Lieutenant. But I'll look."

Johnson turned and walked over to meet Tucker and Alan, who had just gotten out of the patrol car.

"What the hell is going on here?" Johnson demanded, his small eyes studying Alan.

"This is Mr. Alan Avery," Tucker said, ignoring Johnson's remark. "Lieutenant Johnson."

"How do you do," Alan said, extending his hand.

Johnson gave it a limp shake and growled at Tucker. "You know better than to take off like that, Ernie."

"Look, Lieutenant," Tucker said, his hands on his hips. "Do you want to stand here and argue about it, or would you rather listen to Mr. Avery?"

Johnson grunted and the bare outline of a smile curved his fat lips. "Okay, Mr. Avery, let's start from the beginning," he said.

"Just a minute, Lieutenant," Tucker interrupted. "Has anyone gone to pick up Ricca?"

"No rush," Johnson said. "We know where he lives."

"Let me do it, Lieutenant."

"You stick around."

"I'd consider it a personal favor."

"Why?"

"You know why."

"You tell me."

"Forget it," Tucker said, and spun around on his heels.

"Come back here," Johnson said.

Tucker stopped and looked at the lieutenant over his shoulder. "I'm in no mood for games."

"Relax," Johnson said, smiling, his eyes faintly amused. "Have fun."

"Thanks," Tucker said.

"And no rough stuff," Johnson called out after him. "I want him back in one piece. And alive!"

4.

Tucker was driving when he and Cross arrived at the Belvedere Plaza, a plush apartment house on the Sunset Strip. He drove into the subterranean garage and stopped by the attendant's booth. There was a penciled note stuck to the glass informing them that the attendant would be right back. They got out of the patrol car and rode the self-service elevator to the fourth floor. The carpeting in the hallway was like the turf of a golf green, soft and deep. Tucker knocked on 418 and waited. He knocked again, hard and impatient this time.

"My luck," he said gruffly. "Nobody home."

"What do we do now?"

"Go down and wait."

"Christ, we might have to wait all night."

"Yeah."

They went back down to the subterranean garage and

Tucker parked the patrol car in a far corner of the garage, completely out of sight. Then they walked over to the booth and waited for the attendant. Ten minutes later the attendant came back. He was an old man, close to seventy, and he walked as erect as a private in boot camp. He was small, with a sharp face and big eyes that twinkled as he looked at the two officers.

"What can I do you for?" he asked, trying to keep from laughing.

"What's so funny, dad?" Tucker asked, annoyed at the old man for keeping them waiting.

"You guys are funny," he grinned. "Why you ducking so fast when I come in?"

Tucker took out his identification and held it before the man's face. "Where does Ricca park his Cadillac?"

"Mr. Joseph Ricca?" the old man asked, the smile gone from his thin lips.

"Yeah. Mr. Joseph Ricca."

"Why? Is there anything wrong?"

"Look, dad. Just answer the question. Where does he park his car?"

Suddenly the old man looked sad, "He ain't done nothing wrong?"

"For Christ sakes. Where does he park his goddam Cadillac?" Cross barked, shoving his face up to the old man's.

"Now, wait a minute. Don't you try to push me around."

Tucker walked up to the old man and looked at him. "Dad, this is the last time I'm asking you. The next time it's gonna be at headquarters and you're gonna be in a cell. Understand?"

The old man hesitated for a moment, then pointed at an empty stall to his left.

"Okay," Tucker said. "We're gonna wait for him over there. Now when he comes in you just act natural. I'm gonna be watching you. One wrong move and I'm gonna book you as an accessory to murder."

"Murder!" The blue eyes popped out, "You mean Mr. Ricca is a murderer?"

"That's what I mean. Now do we understand each other?"

"Yes, sir," the old man said, snapping to attention.

Tucker smiled for a moment, "What are you, an old GI?"

"Yes, sir. Thirty years with the First Cavalry. Of course, it's mechanized now, you know."

"Yeah, I know," Tucker said. "Now you go about your business as usual. We'll be over there waiting."

There were cars parked on each side of the empty stall and Tucker sat in the back seat of one car while Cross sat in the other. They rolled down their windows and waited.

"I'll tell you something," Tucker said. "I'm willing to bet that Slick Danchik is among the missing."

"Who's Danchik?"

"Danchik was a little punk who got mixed up with the big boys. That was a big mistake. Then he got picked up on a narcotics charge and sang his head off. That was his second mistake, and I'm sure his last."

"You know, I've read something about Ricca. It was in a book about the mafia. It seems that the writer considered Ricca a pretty big man in the syndicate. Not a top leader, but plenty important. The funny part was that the writer thought Marty Kahn was just a clown, but the way I understand it, Ricca works for Kahn."

"Marty Kahn is no clown. He's nuts, but all those jokers are nuts. I haven't met the hood yet that wasn't a mental case. Take Marty Kahn, for instance. Lots of people, respectable people, too, will tell you that Kahn is a gentleman, a heck of a good guy. Why, he'll do anything for you." Tucker gave a short, hard laugh. "All you've got to do to find out differently is to disagree when he wants something. You'll find out how nice a guy he really is, but quick."

"Well, this writer said he wasn't important."

"What do you mean by important?"

"Dangerous, I suppose."

"Would you say that a baby playing with nitroglycerin is dangerous?"

Cross smiled and nodded his head in agreement. He was beginning to like Tucker again.

"That's Marty Kahn. You never know what he's liable to do when he gets excited. He's been arrested on suspicion of murder at least seven times. The D.A. never could make it stick, but there's no doubt that Kahn is a killer. There's only doubt as to how many he's killed and how many he's had killed."

"Well, the writer is all screwed up then."

"I know the book. In some spots it's okay, pretty good in fact, but when he starts theorizing it becomes ridiculous. But don't ever kid yourself about whether there's a mafia or not. Take my word for it. There is. And it's stronger and bigger today than it ever was."

"How about Ricca? Is it true that he works for Kahn?"

"He works with Kahn, not for Kahn. I don't think Ricca would work for anybody, except the syndicate. And Marty Kahn is not the syndicate."

"Does the syndicate operate here in Los Angeles?"

"Not yet. Marty Kahn has kept the syndicate out, but if the rumble I get is true, things are gonna be pretty hot for Kahn. All the way around. Jimmy Gracio is in town and Kahn's protection is pulling out. The heat's on. Kahn hasn't been out of his house for two weeks. Even the Traffic Division's got the word to roust him whenever they spot him. He's out on bail on two different charges right now. Things are closing in fast. And I want to be there to nail the lid shut when it finally drops."

"Who's Jimmy Gracio?"

"He's the mafia organizer. Sets up new territories. Works out of New York. Owns plush hotels in Miami, Las Vegas and Havana. Extortion is his specialty. Muscles his way into big corporations. Just small bites. Three or four per cent. But when you own three or four per cent of three or four dozen corporations, you're in the upper-income brackets. On the surface this is a legitimate income, and Jimmy Gracio is a gentleman. He looks like one of your movie stars, dresses like a playboy, big spender, always smiling, patting people on the back. Smokes big, expensive cigars and goes out with heiresses and celebrities. In short, a real Don Juan. Yet he's been known to throw a tantrum over a traffic citation, and rave like a maniac. Even threatened to have the officer murdered. Two years later, that same policeman was blown to bits one night when he stepped on the starter of his car. Jimmy Gracio was in Havana at the time. You figure it."

Cross stared at Tucker. "You really hate them, don't you?"

"Yes," Tucker said. "I hate them. I hate them with every nerve, every cell in my body. They are the scum of the earth, a threat to every decent man and woman in the world. They're everywhere, waiting to pounce on the weak. And they'll destroy anyone who stands in their way. Yes, Bob, I hate them. And so should you, and anyone with a grain of intelligence should see the danger. I tell you one thing. If everybody hated them the way I do, they wouldn't be around. I'd kill every last one of them."

"Christ! You don't mean that!"

"Yes, I mean it. Now, remember, I'm talking about organized crime. I'm not talking about the petty thief or anyone like that. I'm talking about the hardened criminal who has made crime a big business. The guys who take billions, and I mean billions, away from poor, innocent people every year. The hood who will introduce your kid sister to dope, beat up your brother, or kill your old man whenever he pleases. That's the guy I'm talking about, and that's the guy I want to see dead."

Cross was silent as he stared at Tucker. He could feel the hate with every word, and for a moment he didn't know how to cope with this new Tucker. How do you talk to a man whose eyes become stone, whose face turns into a mask of hatred. He waited while Tucker took out his service revolver and cracked it open. Then he flipped it shut and laid it down on his lap.

"Check your gun," he said, "and be ready for anything. When I give you the word, scoot down and wait until you hear my voice before coming up. Then come up quick. Don't try getting out of the car until I tell you. The guy on your side should be Axe Doto, a fat little slob who's not much good for anything anymore except trotting behind Ricca."

"I was just wondering," Cross said, examining his revolver. "What about that teacher? Isn't he taking a chance? Isn't it dangerous?"

"Yes," Tucker said, looking hard at Cross. "It's dangerous."

"Well," Cross said, "Shouldn't somebody tell him?"

"Why?"

"Christ, the guy ought to know the score."

"Never mind the score. Avery is the best thing that's happened in the last ten years. Now we have a chance to crack this thing wide open."

"What if they kill him?"

"That's the chance we have to take."

"We! What the hell do we have to do with it?"

"We're policemen. That's what we have to do with it."

Just then Tucker saw the nose of the big Cadillac swing through the opened garage door and come to a bouncing stop at the old man's booth.

"Get down!" he called, dropping to the floor of the car. He held the police special in his hand and he slowly tripped back the hammer. He waited, his body tense, his ears straining for the sound of the approaching car. Tucker was a man of action and this, although he wouldn't admit it, was what he enjoyed most in his job. He waited, the gun held steady in his moist hand, anxious for the moment.

Joe Ricca leaned out of the opened window and called to the old man, who was sitting on a high stool within the booth. The old man's eyes were not twinkling now. They were clouded with fear and indecision. He didn't want to leave the imaginary security of the booth.

"Get your ass over here," Ricca called for the third time. "What the hell's wrong with the old son of a bitch?"

The old man just stared at him without moving. His thin, bony hands were clenched tightly together and he could feel the sweat forming inside them. "I don't feel so good," he said, his voice dry and cracking.

Ricca glanced at Doto and shook his head with disgust. "To hell with it," he grunted, and the big Cad leaped forward, tires squealing on the pavement. He swung the wheel sharply and came to a bouncing stop inches from the wall facing the stall.

"You get a pail of water and clean up the trunk."

"Ah, Joe, why can't it wait till morning? Man, I'm dragging."

"That's too goddam bad about you," Ricca said, turning off the ignition. "I want it cleaned tonight. And I want it done right. Understand?"

Doto mumbled some incoherent protest, keeping his big

head down, not wanting to look at Ricca's face. He knew that Ricca was furious. Everything had gone wrong—Danchik's running like some scared rabbit, then getting all that blood in the trunk of the car. And to top it off, Doto had forgotten to bring the shovels. They had had to kick the dirt back into the hole. The whole goddam operation had been loused up. And Doto knew who would have to take the blame for it.

"Okay, Joe," he whined. "I'll clean it good."

Ricca dropped the keys into the side pocket of his suit jacket and pushed the door open. He gave Doto a sharp, meaningful look and slammed the door shut. He had gone about three steps between the two cars before he saw the gun aimed at his head. He stopped short and stared in amazement at Tucker, his hands slowly moving up to his chest.

"Don't be stupid, Joe," Tucker said, and his voice was hard and tense. "Don't make me kill you."

Cross was ready when he heard Tucker's voice. He came up quick, ready for anything. But he could have taken his time. Doto never saw him. He was bending down, looking across at Tucker through the side windows of the Cadillac. Cross pushed the gun barrel against Doto's neck. The fat little man cried out in surprise, jumping back so that the barrel was almost buried into his loose flesh. Then, slowly, he stood erect, his hands automatically going above his head without a single word being spoken.

"Hey, Sergeant," Cross called. "This one's really trained."

"Hold him there," Tucker called back.

"What's the beef?" Ricca demanded, his face flushed, his dark eyes hard and wary.

"Just move over there and take it slow," Tucker ordered, pointing to the back of the car with the gun.

Ricca looked at Tucker and shook his head. "You stupid

clown. I'll get you for this. You wait and see. I'll get you good."

"Shut up and get back there," Tucker ordered. "I don't want any wise talk."

Ricca shrugged his shoulders and started walking to the back of the Cadillac.

"That's far enough," Tucker commanded. "Now turn around and face the other way."

"Drop dead," Ricca said. "Who the hell do you think you're ordering around, you lousy fuzz."

Tucker came out of the car fast, the service special aimed at Ricca's head all the time. He walked up to Ricca and held the gun close to his face.

"One more wise crack and I lay this right across that big, fat, filthy mouth of yours."

Ricca's lips curled up in a menacing grin but he didn't say anything. His eyes just bored into Tucker's, who stared back with even more hatred.

"Okay," Tucker said to Doto, backing away so he could cover both men. "This way, fat boy."

Doto came slouching out, his hands still above his head, his eyes staring at his shoes.

"Stand next to your lord and master here," Tucker said, waving him over with the gun. "Okay, Bob, come on out and cuff these monkeys together."

Cross hurried out and went behind the two men and snapped handcuffs on their wrists.

"Here," Tucker said, tossing him his pair of cuffs. "Get them back to back and snap these cuffs on the other set of wrists."

Ricca swore and spat on the concrete floor.

"And get that gun out of Ricca's shoulder holster. Fine. Now let's have a look in that trunk."

5.

The hearing secretary dropped the pencil on the desk and brushed back the thin strand of hair that had fallen across his forehead while he had hurriedly taken down Alan Avery's statement. He had gotten every word of it down without once asking for the speaker to slow down or repeat a single word. It had been a long statement, too, with plenty of fast questions from Lieutenant Johnson, who liked to keep things rolling at top speed. That Johnson was a hard man, but he was all right. He had his faults, God only knew how many, but he was straight. And that went a long way when you were a cop. Being straight for a cop made up for just about anything in the book. Johnson would push the hell out of you, but he was straight and people excused the method whenever the intentions were good. You couldn't really tell about Johnson, anyway. Sometimes he would become interested in your health and end up giving free medical advice, usually some ancient remedy his great-grandmother had concocted during the Civil War. Other times, he didn't care if you stood on a corner twenty-four hours and froze to death.

The secretary cleared his throat and spoke to Johnson. "Will that be all, Lieutenant?" His voice sounded weak and timid in the quiet room.

Johnson looked across the room and nodded his head. Slowly, the secretary closed his notebook, picked up his pencil, brushed back that same wisp of hair, and stood up. He particularly hated to walk out of a room when everybody was staring at him. It made him feel self-conscious. He wished someone would say something to take the attention away from him. He stood by the desk a moment, fingering the notebook, then taking his courage in hand, he rushed out of the room with a flurry.

Johnson looked at Alan sitting in the straight back chair and smiled, his red, round face lighting up for a moment.

"I want you to know we appreciate what you're doing, Mr. Avery."

"Well, thank you," Alan replied, suddenly feeling awkward.

"You understand, of course, we'll expect you to testify in court to this statement?"

"Yes," Alan said. "Naturally."

"And you have no objection to this?"

"None at all."

"Fine."

Just then there was a knock at the door and a young uniformed policeman came in and handed the lieutenant an envelope. Johnson grunted his appreciation and the officer left as quickly as he had come in. Johnson opened the envelope and took out some photographs.

"Now, Mr. Avery, I wonder if you would look at these pictures. Tell me if you recognize any of these men."

Alan went over each picture slowly, hesitating at the picture of Ricca and Doto long enough for Johnson to notice.

"You recognize these two men?" he asked, after Alan had handed back the photographs and Johnson had taken out the photos of Ricca and Doto and given them back to him.

"I don't know. Maybe if I saw them in person it would be different. It was dark and I couldn't see too well. I'm sorry."

"Don't worry about it. You'll get a chance to see them in person."

The thought of seeing them again was suddenly abhorrent to Alan. It brought back the whole horrible nightmare before his eyes. Especially the part where the knife plunged into the man's throat and the blood gushed out. He felt himself get sick and he fought against the angry growling in his stomach. He swallowed hard and tried to think of something else. Think of Edie and the baby. Maybe it would be a boy. That would be real nice. A girl would be nice, too. Anything would be nice. Anything at all. Just as long as he didn't have to think of that knife. But as hard as he tried, he could not get away from the knife and the blood. It rode over everything else, and finally he gave himself to it, seeing it acted out in his mind, over and over again, until the vomit rose to his throat and he stood up, his hand over his mouth, his eyes wildly searching about. Then Johnson was at his side, directing him to a sink on the other side while his tall, thin body shook with the spasms of retching, until there was nothing left to come up but the thought and the habit and the dry heaves.

Johnson led him back to the straight back chair and Alan sat down stiffly, embarrassed by his weakness.

"I'm sorry," he said, his voice barely audible.

"Forget it," Johnson said. "I've seen all kinds of guys toss their cookies on a lot less than this."

The telephone rang and Johnson went to his desk to answer it. He grunted a couple of times and dropped the receiver back into the cradle.

"That was Tucker. They're bringing in Ricca and Doto."

"Those two men?" Alan asked, his stomach beginning to rumble again.

"Yeah."

"I see. You want me to identify them?"

"We're gonna have a line-up as soon as they get here. We'd appreciate it if you'd try to make an identification."

"I'll do everything I can," Alan said.

"Look, Mr. Avery, maybe I shouldn't say this, but I will anyway. These men are tough; they've been mixed up in crime since they went into long pants. Now it's possible that they might want to get revenge for what you're about to do. You understand, of course, we'll give you all the protection you want, but I think it's only fair that I tell you this. They wouldn't hesitate a minute to kill you if you got in their way and if they thought they could get away with it."

"I see," Alan said, staring at the lieutenant, not actually believing such a thing possible. "But as long as I have police protection I don't see why I have to worry."

Lieutenant Johnson's dull eyes studied Alan for a moment, then looked down at the desk and flipped a switch on the intercom. "Send somebody in here to take Mr. Avery to the line-up room."

Johnson came around the desk and held out his hand. "Thanks," he said. "I'll see you later."

Ricca and Doto's arrival at headquarters was carried out with the utmost secrecy. They were ushered in through the back entrance and hurried up the stairs to homicide on the third floor. Tucker avoided the lobby where the elevators were. He wanted Johnson to have a little time with them before their attorney started breathing down his neck.

Almost immediately, before they had even reached the third floor, a telephone rang in the bedroom of a quarter-million-dollar estate nestled in the pine- and jasmine-scented hills of Bel Air.

A thick, heavy-set man in mauve striped silk pajamas rolled over in bed, away from the silver blonde breathing deeply at his side, and grunted loudly, opening his huge dark eyes, now heavy and swollen with sleep. He reached over to a small table by the bed and picked up the telephone. He spoke into it harshly, then listened briefly.

"What!" he barked, completely awake. "Yeah, yeah,"

he said, and angrily slammed the receiver back on its cradle.

"Jesus H. Christ!" he screamed. "Damn it all to hell, what's going on around here lately? Everything gets loused up good." He was sitting up in the bed now, his pudgy face dark with anger.

"What's the matter?" Marie asked, staring up at him from the luxury of the bed, her silver-blonde hair soft and tousled. "What're you yelling for? You woke me up."

Marty Kahn turned and glared at her. "That's too goddam bad about you," he yelled. "Too goddam bad!"

"Now, Marty, don't talk like that. You promised."

"Shit!"

"Marty!" She sat up in the bed and shook her silver head to indicate the degree of her disappointment.

"Don't give me no trouble," he yelled, pushing her back down roughly. "Go to sleep."

"You're horrible," she screamed.

"I'll be a son of a bitch," he cried, raising his hands in a pleading motion. "Get off my back. I've got enough problems. That goddam LAPD's got Ricca and Doto. Just what I need. Some more bail juice. Christ, I'm bailed up to my eyebrows right now. Why couldn't that son of a bitch stay out of trouble?"

"I'm glad," she said. "I don't like him. He's always leering. He thinks I'm a whore because I live with you and we're not married."

"Oh, for Christ sakes, go back to sleep. I've got to call the doctor."

"Are you sick?"

"You're gonna drive me nuts," he screamed, shaking his fist at her. "You know goddam well who I mean."

"No, I don't," she whimpered, about ready to cry. "Why are you yelling at me? I didn't do nothing."

"I'm gonna call Barker. You know, Bryce Barker, my

goddam lawyer. Now will you go back to sleep and let me think this out."

"He's nice," she said, her baby voice low and sweet, as she sat up in the bed and wrapped her arms around his neck. "Real nice." And she thought of Bryce Barker as she kissed Marty Kahn in the neck, pressing her large firm breasts, covered only by the sheer nylon gown, into his broad back. With her eyes closed she could make believe it was Barker she held in her arms. She lay her head on Marty's shoulder and smiled, her face soft and dreamy as she savored the image.

"Okay, okay," he said, pulling her arms off from his neck, "I've got work to do. So keep them things on ice." He pinched one of her breasts.

She screamed and lashed out at him with both hands, the small hard fists striking his neck. "You're gonna give me cancer," she cried, and quickly slipped the bruised breast out of the gown and examined it, rubbing it gently with her fingertips. "That's a lousy thing to do to a woman. Don't you know that? Boy, you're pretty stupid, all right."

Marty watched her rub the breast, his dark eyes flashing angrily. Marie gave him a quick side glance and went on with the massage. Marty leaned over and picked up the telephone. He dialed Bryce Barker's number and waited. It rang more than fifteen times before he threw the receiver at the cradle and missed. He leaned over and picked it up from the floor and slapped it over the cradle.

"That bastard ought to wear his goddam hearing aid to bed. How the hell does he expect someone to reach him?"

"Maybe he's at Diane's place," Marie volunteered without looking up from her massaging.

"What's her number?"

"I don't know."

"Well, goddam it, drop that and get it."

"For crying out loud," Marie wailed. "You're getting impossible."

Diane Wood sat erect in the middle of the huge circular bed, completely naked, the covers up to her waist. Her small round breasts, firm and pointed, jiggled slightly every time she spoke. There were tears in her blue eyes as she looked at Bryce Barker, who sat in a chair facing the bed, holding a drink in one hand and a cigarette in the other. He was naked except for pale green silk boxer shorts. Being completely deaf in one ear and partially deaf in the other, he wore a hearing aid at all times. Tonight the battery case lay in his lap, the long connecting wire rubbing against his chest whenever he moved his head. It was beginning to annoy him.

"Cut it out," he said. "I'm in no mood for dramatics."

"You don't love me," she said, her voice tense with emotion.

"Love has nothing to do with it," he answered, slurring his words. "So stop being the martyr."

"I love you," she said, starting to get up.

"Don't," he said, waving her back. "One fiasco a night is enough."

She hesitated a moment, then almost timidly, she looked sideways at him. "Are you too old?"

"Goddam!" Barker shouted. "Drop it. Let's not make a DeMille spectacular out of it. So I couldn't. Well, so what? If you want it so bad, find someone else."

"I don't want it," she cried, crushed and insulted. "You have no right to say that. I want you, not it."

"Oh, what the hell," he said, suddenly tired of the whole subject. "It's not you. You're still an appetizing little dish. It's this," and he lifted the drink, staring at the amber liquid. "It dampens the fires of spring," and he smiled for the first time since jumping out of bed earlier, cursing loudly to cover up his failure.

"It's been a long time," she said. "Maybe you should see a doctor."

"Sure," he said, "and get hormone injections. You'd like that, wouldn't you? Then we'd have a sweet old time rattling the bedsprings all night."

"Yes," she said, her voice low and husky. "That's what I want. Like it used to be."

"Sure, sure," he said. "I used to be a big man in bed. Carried a big club. Now I'm a big man in a chair and I carry a big bottle. So, as I said before, if you're interested in bedtime gymnastics, do your shopping somewhere else."

"You're trying awfully hard to hurt me. Does it make you feel better?" She cried, the tears beginning to overflow, her voice getting higher all the time.

"Take it easy," he said. "You're getting manic again."

"I'm not manic," she screamed.

"Sure you are," he said, grinning. "You'll flip for sure one of these days."

"And what are you?" she cried, shaking her head angrily, the raven-black hair flying, the blue eyes snapping, the small breasts propelled into frenzied motion. "Perfectly sane?"

"No," he said, looking at her gravely. "I'm the worst of the worse. It's always worse when you know it. And I've known it a long time."

"I'm sorry," she said. "I didn't mean that."

"Now, take Marty Kahn," he said, ignoring her apology. "He's an advanced case of manic depressive, but he doesn't know it yet. That's different."

"I don't want to hear about that nasty little bastard."

Bryce drained the drink and smiled. "Earn your keep," he said, holding up the glass.

She sat for a moment, composing herself, then slowly

stood up on the bed, her half-covered heavy-lidded eyes warily watching for his reaction. She stood completely naked, her tall, slim, mature body frozen in the soft pink light of the bedroom.

Then slowly she walked across the huge bed, her narrow, boyish hips swaying seductively with the sinking of each foot in the deep foam-rubber mattress. Barker watched without interest. She stopped at the edge of the bed and glanced back at him before stepping down. He noticed how firm her buttocks were, how little they shook as she walked out of the room. But it didn't do a damn thing for him.

He lit another cigarette and tried to relax. Thinking about Marty Kahn always boosted his blood pressure, made him tense and short-tempered. Ten years was a long time to be associated with a bastard like Marty Kahn. It didn't seem possible that it had been that long. Ten years of his life spent defending hoods and thugs.

It had all started when he was just fresh out of law school. Marty and Ricca were launching their careers. They were arrested and charged with tearing out telephone equipment from the old wire-service center, and with assault on big Jim McCarthy, the operator of the place. Barker heard about it and volunteered his services, because he knew he could get the case dismissed.

From then on it was inevitable. Small jobs gradually grew in scope and importance as Marty grew in stature, until finally Bryce was devoting himself completely to Marty's many and varied enterprises.

She came back with the drink and he took it from her as she leaned over to kiss him hard on the mouth. She tried to press against him and he brushed the cold, wet glass against her breasts. She jumped back, startled, her face struggling to control the anger that flashed in her eyes.

Barker reached over and pulled angrily at the wire connecting the receiver in his ear to the battery case on his lap. The little round plastic ball came bouncing out of his ear and down his chest. He picked up the contraption and dropped it to the carpeted floor. It felt good to be rid of that nuisance, to sit like any other normal person. He stretched out his legs and raised the drink to his lips. She was standing before him, her small pointed breasts mutely staring at him.

"Get back to bed," he snapped.

She went back reluctantly, frowning, her full mouth set hard, but the rest of her completely at ease in nudity.

"Screw you," she said, settling herself in the center of the bed again with the blankets wrapped around her waist. "You deaf bastard."

Barker saw her lips move but didn't try to read them. He raised the glass and swallowed deeply, feeling the cool liquid burn on the way down. He remembered how quickly he had pegged Kahn as a psycho. He had gone back to his school texts and had easily found Kahn's psychological pigeonhole. Even physically he fitted the picture of a manic depressive. He was short, stocky and had a thick neck. This was what Kretschmer had classified as the pyknic type. Emotionally, he fitted the syndrome perfectly. He couldn't sit still for a second, always had to be doing something, usually flitting from one thing to another, clowning, showing off, and butting into other people's business, always the center of attraction, monopolizing the conversation, giving freely of his views on all topics with dogmatic bluntness and complete intolerance of criticism. He was rude and sarcastic with anyone who disagreed with him no matter what it was about or who it was. Lately he had been extremely irritable, domineering, more cruel than usual.

Barker expected him to slip by that thin dividing line

between hypomania and acute mania. As far as Barker was concerned, Kahn was not long for the outside world. There was a padded cell waiting for him in some nice institution. What worried Barker was what Kahn would do before the men in the white coats carted him off to that nice institution. Working for Marty Kahn today was like waiting for a time bomb to go off and not knowing for what time it had been set.

Barker was lost deep in thought when the telephone rang and Diane handed him the receiver. He looked up, startled, almost surprised to see her, then replaced his hearing aid and spoke into the instrument. He listened a while, nodding his finely shaped head, his handsome face inscrutable.

Marty Kahn was doing the talking and there wasn't much chance for interruption.

"Christ, you know how Joe is about these things, I want him out right away."

"All right," Bryce said. "I'll do what I can."

"Never mind that crap. Get him out. Now!"

"Look, Marty, I don't know the score yet. As far as I know they might be up for murdering the police commissioner."

"Cut the clowning. For Christ sakes, Joe's in trouble and needs our help. Let's give it to him. Get going."

"Okay, don't get in a sweat. I'm on my way. What's the beef?"

"How the hell would I know? Go down and find out. It's that goddam LAPD. Those bastards are out to get me. I'm telling you this is just another roust. Listen, Doctor, I need Joe. I need him bad. The whole works is blowing sky-high. And after all the goddam juice I've spread around this stinking town. I can't figure it. All the goddam protection has vanished."

"Okay, Marty. I'm on my way. Take it easy, will you?"

"Take it easy my ass. Somebody's got to do the worrying around this place. I'm telling you the whole goddam organization is going up in smoke. And me with a million bucks invested in this town. Well, let me tell you something. I don't intend to see this dough blow away. You hear me!"

"Yes, I hear you. I'm on my way."

"And don't forget. That means your hundred grand per annum. When Marty Kahn goes down, every one of you bastards will end up in the gutter. So you better get the goddam lead out and get some action around here. Earn your goddam money."

"Marty, if you don't get off this phone I'll never get Joe out."

"The hell with Joe. That stupid son of a bitch should know enough to stay out of trouble. Christ, he knows the heat's on."

"Okay," Barker said.

"Get your ass down there, Doctor. And don't forget to call me. I can't sleep a damn with all this trouble."

"I'll call you," Barker said, quickly hanging up before Kahn had a chance to get started again.

"How was Marty Manic?" Diane asked, handing him his trousers. She was wearing a red nylon negligee that did plenty for what it hid even though what it hid was no secret any more.

"I think he's about ready to slip into a dark, deep depression. The whole world is against him, plotting and scheming just to annoy him. And he's been so good to everybody."

Barker stood up and weaved slightly as he tried to slip a foot into the trouser leg, then hopped around madly on one foot, trying to regain his balance. He hit the side of the bed and fell across it. Angrily, he looked up and saw Diane laughing, and then, slowly at first, he began to laugh.

She ran to him, throwing herself on top of him, pressing down hard with her full, firm body. Then they were looking deep into each other's eyes, not more than inches apart, and he found himself staring into the magic of those dark blue, almost purplish, eyes, now disappearing under slowly closing eyelids, eyelids decorated with the longest, darkest, most beautifully curved eyelashes he had ever seen. He watched as her now sightless face moved closer to his and suddenly the urge that had been dormant for so long came to life and he felt it stir all through his body. Felt himself go weak, go strong. And she felt it and pressed hard, her whole body moving against his, and he kissed her, hard and furious, feeling her teeth cut into his lip, and he pressed up against her and she pressed down, and the whole world stopped and only they soared forward and outward and upward.

6.

Alan Avery made a tentative identification at the line-up. Everything had happened quickly. The men, eight of them, had walked onto a small stage and the lights above and below the stage had bathed them in a white glare. An old, uniformed policeman had spoken into a microphone connected to a P.A. system, calling out directions. Alan stood in the dark room, staring at the white, glaring stage, listening to the old policeman and to Lieutenant Johnson, both men speaking at the same time.

"Face the front, stand erect ..." the old policeman was saying.

"Take your time," Johnson was saying. "Don't worry about it if you don't recognize them ..."

"You, there, in the middle, raise your head, show your

face …"

"Just take your time. Look 'em over good …"

"What's your name? Speak up …"

"Watch each one as they come forward … listen to 'em when they talk …"

"Come on, move. Get the lead out …"

Finally Ricca and Doto stepped forward and Alan identified them. The only trouble was that he didn't know if he recognized them from the parking lot or from the pictures he had seen in Johnson's office. He told this to Johnson and was told not to worry about it. Johnson was more interested in the physical identification, shape and form, than in the facial. Alan was positive about the physical. The tall, broad-shouldered man and the short, fat man with the big head. That much of it fit perfectly. And then, of course, there was the license number and the fact that the men were known criminals. Put all the pieces together and it made for the best kind of identification. Johnson was satisfied.

They came out of the line-up room to face a battery of bursting flashbulbs and a barrage of questioning reporters. As usual, the word had gotten to the newspapers and they hadn't lost any time in getting there. Johnson stood beside Alan, answering some questions, ignoring others. Alan told them his name and address and that he was a teacher at Hollywood High School. That did it. They closed in around him, ignoring Johnson.

"Ever heard of Ricca before?" one of the reporters asked.

"No."

"How about Marty Kahn?"

"Vaguely."

"Are you worried about your safety?"

"I don't understand?"

"Revenge, Mr. Avery. Aren't you afraid they might want

to get even with you for turning them in?"

"I've been promised police protection if I want it."

"Are you going to ask for police protection?"

"No. I don't think so." The reporter noticed the angry look that quickly swept over Johnson's face.

"Are you married?" he asked, changing his line of questions.

"Yes."

"Any children?"

"No. But we expect one momentarily."

There was some laughter among the group and Alan smiled for the first time that evening.

Johnson cleared his throat and started walking away from the reporters.

"That's enough for now, fellows. Mr. Avery is tired and I've got work to do."

"How about talking to Ricca and Doto?" they asked.

"Not now," Johnson said. "I'll let you know later if anything develops."

The photographers asked for a couple more pictures and Johnson waited impatiently for them to finish. After the reporters and photographers had left, Johnson thanked Alan and sent him home in a patrol car.

Sam Johnson knew Joe Ricca only too well. Ricca had been in and out of Homicide at least a dozen times in the past ten years. Each time the case had looked promising and each time Ricca had been released for insufficient evidence. Witnesses had the bad habit of going deaf, dumb and blind whenever it concerned Ricca and Kahn. This time, though, Johnson believed it would be different.

For reasons he couldn't quite understand, since lifelong habits had made him wary of all witnesses, he had taken a strong liking to Alan Avery. Avery, he thought, could be depended upon to do his duty as a citizen even in the face of danger. He knew that he was being irrational in his reasoning. There was absolutely nothing in Avery's behavior to warrant this belief. As a matter of fact, Avery was soft. The sight of violence had made him ill. This wasn't the kind of man who stood up and defied vicious killers. Yet, as he sat behind his gray steel desk, studying Ricca and Doto, who sat on straight-back chairs facing him, he could feel the confidence rising, and he smiled slightly, just the bare outline of a smile curving his thick lips. No one except Tucker, who stood with Cross behind Ricca and Doto, noticed the smile.

"I wanna call Barker," Ricca was saying.

"Later," Johnson said, almost startled out of his thoughts. "First I want to hear your story."

"There ain't no goddam story."

"Why's the Axe sweating?"

Doto took out an expensive linen handkerchief and mopped his wet forehead.

"It's hot," Doto said.

"You're not kidding there, fat boy," Tucker said, leaning over the back of the chair to face Doto. "And it's gonna be a lot hotter before it's over."

"Get off my back."

"You know what happens to killers in this state?"

"I didn't kill nobody."

"Yeah. We've got a witness that says you did. Saw you. Was right there when you slit Danchik's throat."

"Yeah? Well, he's crazy!"

"What did you do with the body?"

"Nothing," Doto shouted, his flabby face red and wet. "There's no body."

"How did you get all that blood in the car?"

"Shut up, Axe," Ricca shouted, spinning around in the chair so fast that his shoulder struck Tucker on the side of the head. "You're deaf and dumb from now on. Remember that!"

Doto's big head came down against his chest with a jolt, his small eyes fixed on the buttons of his suit jacket.

Tucker straightened up and rubbed his head where Ricca's shoulder had struck it. If Johnson hadn't been in the room he would have taken Ricca apart but quick. He was sure that Ricca had done it on purpose. He looked down at the top of Ricca's head, at the black, greasy hair, and the hatred flowed through his blood like a wild passion. He wanted to strike out with his big fist, right on top of that greasy head, hit until the hatred turned that hideous head to a pulp. He looked up and saw Johnson's colorless eyes studying him. He returned the look for a moment, then looked back down again at the top of Ricca's head. The moment of passion had passed. There was only a dull hatred left.

Johnson spoke. "Answer the question, Axe. What did you do with the body?"

Doto kept his head down, his fat lips pressed tightly together.

Tucker slapped him hard on the neck. "Answer the lieutenant," he barked.

Doto's head didn't move. His eyes blinked a couple of times and that was all the reaction Tucker got.

"Well," Johnson said. "Maybe we need a little change here. Ernie, you take Doto into the other room. Have a talk with him."

Tucker looked at Johnson and smiled. "That's a good idea."

Ricca smiled ruefully. "Just remember, Axe. Deaf and dumb."

Doto nodded his big head, his small eyes still fixed on the buttons.

"Okay, fat boy, let's go," Tucker said, gripping the Axe's shoulder, almost lifting him out of the chair. Doto stood up and went out of the room, Tucker close behind him.

"Let's have it, Ricca," Johnson said, after the door closed.

Ricca settled back in the chair and smiled.

"Well," Johnson said. "I ain't got all night."

Ricca crossed his leg, pulling up the trouser leg to protect the sharp crease. "You surprise me, Lieutenant," he said, smiling pleasantly. "You know I once heard some character on radio give a definition for intelligence. He said it was the ability to learn from experience."

"Very interesting," Johnson said.

"Yeah, I thought so. Now take you, for example. You're a police lieutenant, you're supposed to be intelligent, and yet every time we go through the same routine. Why don't you learn from experience, Lieutenant?"

Tucker sat on a straight chair facing Doto, who hadn't spoken a word in the five minutes they had been in the room. Tucker realized how frightened Doto was of Ricca, and this made it difficult. There was nothing he could threaten Doto with that was as bad as Ricca.

"Look, Axe," he said, his voice now soft and sympathetic. "I know you're afraid of Ricca. But what can Ricca do to you if he's in jail? We've got him cold. We've got an eyewitness. A respectable schoolteacher saw the whole thing. You couldn't possibly ask for a better witness, now could you? He saw you guys chasing Danchik, saw Danchik climb on top of the car and he saw Ricca cut his throat. He saw you bring the car around and load the body in the trunk. He took the license number and that's how you're here. He's just identified you in the line-up. What more do you think we need? Now, if you talk, tell us where the body is buried, then we probably could make a deal with you; otherwise you'll both get the gas chamber. I'm not kidding. This is it. This is the one that finishes you guys off. You bums go on for years committing crimes. Then one day something happens, just like tonight, and you're finished. So how about it, Axe? You want to cooperate and save your own neck?"

Doto kept his head down, his lips sealed tightly together, his small eyes buried in his big head.

Tucker glared at him. "Where's the body?" he shouted. "You stupid jerk, don't you have enough sense to save your filthy hide. I'm giving you that chance. You oughta wise up, punk. Can't you read the handwriting on the wall? Ricca is finished. All done. And I'm giving you a chance to save yourself. Wise up before it's too late."

Two minutes after Bryce Barker arrived at headquarters he knew the whole story. This time Ricca had really loused things up. At first he thought of calling Kahn and telling him, but he decided against it. He had enough trouble right now without asking for more. He took the elevator to the third floor and went into Homicide. Six or seven policemen were standing around talking when he came into the room. They stopped and looked at him. One of the policemen, a tall, good-looking man, detached himself from the others and approached Barker.

"Well, Counselor," he said. "You've finally got one cut out for you. Now we'll see how good you are."

Barker smiled and looked at the other officers, who had been listening. "Where are they?" he asked.

"In with the lieutenant. Been there at least an hour. What kept you?"

"How about going in?" Barker asked, walking toward the door of Johnson's office.

"No dice," the officer said, standing in front of Barker. "The lieutenant likes privacy. You know, he's sort of queer that way."

"I want to see my clients."

"No can do," the officer said.

"What the hell goes on here?" Barker demanded, getting angry.

"Nothing, Counselor. What do you think goes on?"

"I want to see my clients."

"Tough titty," the officer said, and they all laughed. "Your clients are in conference. Can't be disturbed."

"What are you, the local comedian?"

"That's right, Counselor. I learned all those jokes walking a beat on Central. Don't you remember, your boss arranged it for me. Nice fella, that Marty Kahn. Used to have a lot of suction. Too bad it all went down the drain."

"I don't think there's anything more pathetic than a wise-cracking cop," Barker said, glaring at him. "I'll have them out on a writ in two hours," he said, not believing a word of it, and turned around and walked out before the good-looking cop could think of an answer.

7.

The Averys lived on the second floor of a duplex apartment on Bonita Avenue in Hollywood. It was a small apartment with an L-shaped living-dining room combination, kitchen and bedroom. The bathroom was the only room the Averys did not think was too small. It was a large room with a sunken tub and separate shower stall, twin cabinet sinks, and all of it finished in a gaudy pink and black tile that reached almost to the ceiling. In the seven years that they had occupied the apartment, they had come to regard it with a feeling of pride and ownership as if it were their home. Slowly, they had been able to furnish it with good modern furniture that they both loved. It was not too expensive, except for one McCobb chair they had purchased in a moment of weakness, but it was all strong and sturdy and functional, with straight simple lines that would be in style for years to come.

Furnishing the apartment had taken a long time, but it had been fun. They had saved a little from each pay check and whenever they had enough accumulated, they went out and bought another piece. Now, the apartment was completely furnished, and the little that came out of each pay check went into the bank to await the arrival of the baby. They had already bought the crib and bathinette and had rearranged the bedroom to accommodate these new pieces. There also was a new chest of drawers painted pink with blue decals of rabbits and various farmyard animals.

When Alan came out of the bathroom that morning, Edie was sitting at the dining table, reading the newspaper. Her face looked pinched and tired. Her dark brown hair was pulled back into a thick, luxurious pony tail that despite the pregnancy and her thirty-one years still made her look like a teen-ager.

She had been awake when he had come in that night, and he had tried to explain to her why he was doing it, why it was important for him to cooperate with the police, to do his duty as a citizen should in a society governed by laws.

And he had tried to tell her that there was no danger, that the criminals were in prison and would stay there, that even if they got out, the police would protect him against harm. She had listened to him, her eyes grave, unbelieving. The police couldn't protect him, she had said. Nobody could really protect him if the criminals wanted to kill him. He couldn't live with a policeman at his side twenty-four hours a day. And even if he could, policemen were not God. They, too, could be killed. The argument had gone on for most of the night and nothing had been resolved.

Edie looked up when he came into the living room and

she smiled a warm, tender smile.

"Good morning," he said, happily, going to the table to kiss her.

"Good morning, darling," she said, taking his kiss, her eyes closing, her arms holding his head down a moment longer than the usual morning kiss.

"What's for breakfast?" he asked, sitting down next to her.

"This morning, you get a big, hot bowl of oatmeal. I'm out of eggs."

"Sounds good," he said, glancing at the newspaper in her hands.

She caught the glance and smiled. "You made the front page, but I'm not sure I like the pictures. You look so grim."

"I felt pretty grim," he said.

"Here," she said, handing him the paper. "I'll get your oatmeal. How many toasts do you want?"

"Oh, two will be fine."

He watched her walk into the kitchen and wondered why she had tried so hard to avoid the subject. Last night she had been almost hysterical. This morning, she was calm and composed. He shook his head, his eyes puzzled, and opened up the newspaper.

The headline ran across eight columns at the top of the front page in bold black type:

TEACHER FINGERS GANGSTERS

And under that in a two-column sub-head:

BRUTAL ATTACK ON MAN SEEN AS 'REVENGE';
POLICE BELIEVE MISSING WITNESS IS VICTIM

Alan looked up from the paper and glanced into the

kitchen. Edie was standing in front of the small white gas stove, stirring the cooking oatmeal, watching him, her large brown eyes worried. She tried to smile when she caught his look but nothing happened. Her facial muscles refused to obey. Slowly, she turned back to the stove and quickened her stirring of the oatmeal.

Alan turned back to the newspaper and began reading the story, his eyes moving quickly over the words, finding a strange detachment in the wording about himself. It was like any other morning. It was the newspaper and the people it told about were strangers, just people you read about. People you didn't know and never would know, because the world you lived in was small. Just one block, and even then, you didn't know one tenth of the people living there with you.

It was a long story, dwelling on the sensational details of the murder. Alan's eyes lingered on two paragraphs:

> Both Ricca and Doto are registered as ex-convicts. Ricca's record traces all the way back to the investigation of Brooklyn's Murder, Inc., where he was held on a murder charge. Ricca has been arrested twenty-two times in Los Angeles on charges of assault, robbery, burglary, narcotics, extortion, pandering and murder.
>
> Ricca's attorney, Bryce Barker, said he applied for a writ of habeas corpus. The writ is returnable in four days. "Unless the police find the so-called body now specified in the charges, my clients will have to be released when the writ is returned."

Edie came in and placed the steaming bowl of oatmeal in front of Alan, then sat down across from him at the dining table. He put down the paper and looked up at her, smiling.

"Eat your cereal before it gets cold," she said.

"Did you read the story?" he asked.

"Yes."

"You know, this Barker, the attorney for Ricca, I think I know him. It's the strangest thing. I used to know a Bryce Barker back home in Keene, New Hampshire."

"Was he a lawyer?"

"Not then. But he left town when he was only nineteen. There was quite a tragedy. His father committed suicide. Climbed up on the church steeple, stayed up there I think almost forty-eight hours before jumping. Barker was at Yale then on a scholarship. He came home, I remember, and tried to talk his father into coming down. Even climbed up the steeple, but the old man wouldn't come down. As I remember it, Barker left town right after the funeral. Never went back to Yale. The story was in all the papers. Became a national item.

"Barker was deaf. Used to carry one of those box speaker things around all the time. Placed it on the teacher's desk and ran a wire to his chair so he could hear. I remember kids used to trip over the wire. Barker was very self-conscious about it. It used to embarrass him to have to carry the thing around. Some of the kids made fun of him. It was pretty awful. You know how mean kids can be. He couldn't afford a good hearing aid, and he used to talk about it all the time. Real bright fellow. We were pretty good friends all through high school. Unfortunately, his hearing impairment became almost a social disease with him. He never went out on dates. Stayed pretty much to himself. Brilliant. Got a full scholarship to Yale. Had the highest grades ever received at Keene High School."

"I don't see how it could be the same person," Edie said, taking a sip of coffee. "He wouldn't be associating with criminals."

"I suppose you're right. It was just the name. You know,

it's not too common. Oh, well, I'm sure you're right." He put sugar and cream in his cereal and started to eat.

Edie watched him eat, looking at him as though she had never seen him before. What she saw was a tall, thin man over six-two tall and perhaps fifty pounds underweight. She looked at the light hazel eyes under the heavy dark eyebrows and was conscious of the low hairline and the thick, crew-cropped dark hair. His face was thin and sensitive. His lips were full and his mouth generous, disclosing white, even teeth when he talked or smiled. The only part of his face that was the least incongruent and insensitive was his nose. It was strong, almost rugged, with a small bump that twisted the broad bridge slightly to one side. Usually, like at the present moment, Alan wore a serious, intelligent expression that was somewhat grim, and then he would smile and his whole face would light up, giving him an almost boyish look. But it was the nose, she thought, that gave his face so much character. That took it out of the ordinary handsome-face category.

He noticed her watching him and he wondered when she would ask the really important question. The one he couldn't answer.

And as if she had read his mind, she said, her voice low and soft. "What were you doing in the parking lot?"

He stopped eating, placed his spoon down on the table, and picked up his coffee. "Well," he said, taking a sip of the hot coffee, "I had been running and ... and I got a cramp in my stomach." He put the coffee cup down and looked at her and smiled reassuringly. "I'm not as young as I used to be. When you get to be thirty-five you can't run like a kid."

"What kind of a cramp?" she asked, her tired eyes worried.

"Oh, you know. The usual thing. It kind of made me a little sick."

"How long were you in the parking lot?"

"How long?"

"The paper says the man was killed around two o'clock. You left here before one. Were you in the parking lot all that time?"

"I guess so," he said. "But it was just a cramp, believe me."

"Alan!" and she was across the table, kneeling down by his chair. "There's nothing wrong with you, is there? You're not keeping anything from me, are you?"

"No, I'm not," he said, running his fingers over her hair. "Please, don't start worrying about that now. There's nothing wrong. I swear it."

"Oh, Alan," and tears came into her eyes. "What's going to happen to us?"

"Nothing," he said. "Don't cry, please."

"I'm not," she said, trying to smile, fighting against the tears that clouded her eyes. For a moment it looked as if she'd be all right, then the small face trembled and there was a quivering along the delicate jaw-line. She looked up at him bravely and he felt his heart tightening. Suddenly the whole brave face collapsed, twisting oddly, going all wrong. She lowered her head, and bit down hard on her lip, and before he could speak through the lump in his throat, her head fell on his lap, and he felt her flesh leaping and shuddering under his hand. She cried like that for a long time, with Alan leaning down over her, his face buried into the fresh scent of that luxurious brown hair. He waited for her to stop, feeling each shudder and sob telegraphed up his long thin legs to his heart and he, too, wanted to cry. Cry for everything that had been so good, and for everything that had gone so wrong, so quickly. He wanted to cry, but he couldn't. Because everything seemed so unreal, so unlike anything that had ever happened to him, that he still wasn't sure that it was actually happening.

"Alan" she said, and the vibration of her voice sent shivers up his legs. "Couldn't you tell them you're not sure?"

The question took him by surprise. Slowly, he raised her head so that she was facing him. "I couldn't do that, honey. You know I couldn't do that."

"If not for me, then please, Alan, do it for the baby."

"No," he said. "I couldn't do it. And besides, it's too late. I gave them the license number and everything. They wouldn't believe me."

"Please, Alan, couldn't you try?"

"No. Don't ask me to do that. I just couldn't."

Slowly, she stood up and stared at him. This was not the Alan Avery she had known for over twelve years. The man she had married and loved so dearly. This was a stranger, a complete, total stranger, someone speaking a foreign tongue, a language she could not understand. The ties of communication had been broken and she felt helpless. She wanted so much to tell him of her fears, of the danger that loomed above them, but she couldn't communicate. He didn't understand her language. Her own fears about the baby were completely forgotten. Now her fears were for Alan and his safety. She knew that she sounded melodramatic at times, like in some cheap gangster movie, but she also knew that she was right. That gangsters did kill people. Good, kind, innocent, law-abiding people. All kinds of people. All you had to do was read the morning paper. Any morning.

That was the thing that puzzled her most about Alan. He read the papers, read about crime and corruption, but he never seemed to associate it to living people. To him all men in public life were honest and upstanding, doing their level best for the government and society as a whole. He refused to believe bad about anybody. He lived in a clean and honest world, anything to the contrary notwithstanding.

"I'm sorry, Alan," she said, now calm and composed again. "I had no right to ask you that. I promise not to mention it again." She looked so small and brave standing there, he was proud her. He stood up and took her in his arms and brought her face up to his.

"I love you," he said. "I love you very much."

She smiled and raised herself on tiptoes, her lips slightly parted, reaching up to him. He leaned down, his mouth closing over hers, and pressed down hard, feeling her lips open under the pressure. Suddenly she broke away, laughing a little timidly.

"You better get ready. Ralph will be here any minute now."

The desire was still strong in him, but he smiled, his white even teeth reflecting the sunlight streaming through the partly opened venetian blinds.

"He's four minutes late already," he said, going into the bedroom for his suit jacket. He came out, buttoning the jacket, and picked up an old leather briefcase from the small modern desk that stood in one corner of the living room. This was where he prepared his assignments and corrected the exam papers. It was his private office. There was a small bookshelf on the wall above the desk and a three-drawer gray steel filing cabinet stood next to the desk.

He worked there evenings while Edie sat on the sofa a few feet away, knitting or reading. Their one big luxury had been a high-fidelity radio. They had bowght all the components and Alan had designed and built the cabinet himself. It was a handsome piece and gave a full rich tonal sound that was unequalled by factory-made sets costing five times as much. They enjoyed all kinds of music, particularly modern classical composers and Jazz. Edie played the hi-fi all day long and there was always music at night, even when Alan was hard at work on his assignments. The music never interfered with his work. It had become part of him. During the summer they went to the Hollywood Bowl for the moonlight concerts, and sat in the fifty-cent section and had as much fun as any high-school kids out on a date.

Edie heard the familiar sound of Ralph Henning's horn outside and came quickly forward for her parting kiss. She smiled at him, not as bravely as she wished, and he smiled and took her hand in his and bent down to kiss her.

"Take it easy today," he said, opening the door. "If you get any labor pains, get Mrs. Murphy to drive you over to St. Luke's. And don't forget to call me."

"Don't worry, I won't forget."

"Okay, little mother, see you later." He pinched her cheek gently and ran down the stairs to Henning's waiting car.

"Bye," she called softly, waving until the car had disappeared around the corner.

Ralph Henning taught Manual Arts at Hollywood High School. He had started out as a physical education major, but his lack of prowess on the football field had made that future look pretty doubtful. In his senior year he had changed his major and spent an extra semester earning the necessary credits. After twenty years of teaching manual arts, Henning still hated it, and still tried each year at contract time to get assigned to the physical ed. department.

He followed all sports, national and local, and his greatest pleasure came during the summer vacation when he supervised a boys' camp in the mountains north of Lake Tahoe. All conversation with Henning gravitated around sports.

Alan particularly enjoyed Henning's Monday morning quarterback sessions, when Henning dissected every important play executed the preceding weekend in the Pacific Coast league and the Big Ten.

On Friday mornings, like today, he would make detailed predictions and quote the exact score, including games won by field goals and once or twice he even threw in a safety. Amazingly enough, a team did win last year by a safety exactly as Henning had predicted. Henning never got over it and Alan never stopped hearing about it.

This morning, though, Henning was not thinking about the football scores for that weekend. He had read the newspaper at breakfast and he was anxious to learn every detail. Alan had barely gotten a foot into the car when he started in on the murder.

"Holy cow," he yelped, "imagine me, little Ralphie, driving a celebrity to work. Front page of the *Los Angeles Tribune*. Picture there big as life. Boy, was Mabel and me surprised when we opened up that old paper this morning. 'Lateral that paper over here, Mabel,' I said, and jeez, just as she went to snap it down the line, it opened and she looked, and boy! Did she gasp. 'Look out for that blocker,' I said, but she wasn't listening. She just stood there staring. Well, you know me, I dug in the old cleats and took off to provide interference. But it was too late. The gun had gone off. The game was over. I looked and saw that kisser of yours and I just about flipped the old helmet.

"Well, let me tell you, buddy boy, you've got guts—spelled in big fat capital letters. Boy, I would have done some fancy broken-field running out of that place. I tell you, buddy, it would have taken the old galloping ghost himself to catch up with me. I give you credit. You've got guts."

Alan grinned and didn't know why. There was really

nothing to grin about. This fat man, sitting next to him, the same fat man he had ridden to work with for the past seven years, was actually telling him the facts of life. In his own picturesque way, he was telling Alan exactly what Edie had tried to tell him. The same thing that Johnson had hinted at in his office, and the same thing the reporters had asked. Each in his own way, but each saying exactly the same thing.

"I had no choice," Alan said, feeling he had to make an excuse. "I was ill and it happened so fast I didn't have time to run."

"Well, I'm telling you, buddy boy, I'd have to be pretty dang sick to stick around there very long. And that part about telling the police, that's the part I admire. That really took guts."

"Why?"

"You know why. Holy cow, everybody knows why."

"I don't," Alan said.

"Gads, boy, those guys would just as soon blow a hole through you as look at you. Don't you know that?"

"They're in jail," Alan said. "How can they kill me?"

"They've got friends. Take that Marty Kahn. That's Ricca's boss. He's not in jail, you know. He's got a big operation. Boy, that guy's always in trouble. Why just two years ago, I think it was, there was a gang war right up there on Sunset. This Marty Kahn came out of one of them fancy nightspots and some guys let go with machine guns. Killed four innocent bystanders, and all that Kahn got was a bullet in the ass. Yeah, that's right. Everybody gets killed and he gets a bullet in the ass.

"Then it was just about a year ago, some guys went into his dry-cleaning plant and shot up the whole place. This time two of his hoods were killed, but he didn't even get a scratch. He was in the bathroom washing his hands. And then, you know, just about a week ago some characters threw a bomb in his front yard and busted every window in the neighborhood. But nothing happened to Kahn, he was out in the back yard having a swim in his pool. The bomb didn't even break his windows. That guy's like one of them cats with nine lives. Why, just a week before the bombing, some hoods were waiting for him when he drove home. Opened up with shotguns, busted his windshield all to shreds, but not one of them little pellets touched him. You know, it's pretty incredible."

"I didn't know that," Alan said, surprised that all that had been going on in Los Angeles.

"Don't you read the newspapers?"

"Sure. But I don't remember reading that."

"Was in all the papers. Every bit of it. Well, as I was saying, this Ricca's got friends that don't appreciate his being in jail. They're the ones to worry about. You wait and see. You'll hear from them."

"I hope not," Alan said, suddenly feeling the gravity of the situation. Until now, he hadn't really thought of himself as being in actual danger. The sharpest thing on his mind had been the murder itself. Every time he had closed his eyes during the night, that scene with the knife had been re-enacted with all the violence and horror that he had felt at that moment. It was as if it had been painted on the inside of his eyelids.

Now it seemed that his own life had been placed in jeopardy. It was a strange thought, to think of one's self in danger, even grave danger, when nothing but words created it. Somehow, he just couldn't work himself up to a feeling of fear. It wasn't real and therefore he couldn't accept it, much less feel it.

"You don't seem much worried," Henning said, sensing Alan's passive attitude.

"Oh, yes," Alan said, not wanting to appear quixotic. "I'm worried."

8.

For the past three weeks, since being transferred to patrol, Sergeant Ernie Tucker read the evening paper when the first edition came out at about eight-thirty in the morning. He read it at his favorite café while he ate his way through half a dozen poached eggs, thick slices of ham, stacks of pancakes and an urn of coffee. Tucker had a good appetite, and like many people with good appetites, he was a slow eater. He liked to sit at a table, relaxed, his paper folded and propped against the napkin dispenser, and leisurely read and eat.

This morning Tucker was in a hurry. He had only two eggs and one slice of ham. No pancakes. Two cups of coffee. He hurriedly read the front-page story about Ricca, then folded the paper.

Rita, the waitress, came over with more coffee but he placed his hand over his cup and shook his head.

"Losing your appetite?" she asked.

"I'm in a hurry this morning."

"Big night?"

"Big enough."

"Looks like another smoggy day," she said, searching for a common interest.

"Yes," he said, standing up. He was wearing a dark brown gabardine suit. He always changed into civilian clothes when he came off duty. "It looks like another red alert."

"My God," she said. "It's certainly awful on my sinus."

"It's pretty bad, all right," he said, signing the check. "Well, see you later," and he hurried out of the café.

All night, since he had talked with Alan Avery, there had been a scheme forming at the back of his mind. He knew he had to get off patrol. And he knew that his chances of getting off were pretty slim unless he could do something about it himself.

He remembered his conversation with Johnson that morning after Ricca and Doto were locked up. They had sat in Johnson's office, drinking coffee, relaxing, just the two of them, when Tucker had confronted Johnson with his problem.

"What can I do about Finch?" he had asked.

"Oh," Johnson had said, his eyes studying Tucker. "Putting me on the spot, eh?"

"Look, Sam," Tucker said. "I've know you a long time and I know how you feel about corruption. Finch is crooked and you know it. You know what he did to me. What can I do about it?"

"Ernie, I'm not gonna tell you what to do, but I will tell you what I'd do if I were in your shoes. You know, Ernie, only an idiot fights fair in a dirty fight. The only way to fight a dirty fighter is to be even dirtier. Get what I mean?"

"Okay, how do I do it?"

"If it was me, I'd tap his phone. I'd tap Marsha Brown's phone. I'd take pictures if I could get them together. I'd really pin them to the canvas. I'd get the kind of evidence the chief would have to listen to. But I wouldn't go to the chief with it. I'd go to Captain Martin of Intelligence. He's a real straight guy. Let him take it to the chief."

Tucker smiled. "Who would you get to tap the phones?"

"Well," Johnson said, scratching his head. "There's a little creep by the name of Merkle who's done a lot of work for us. This is a real character. Works for Kahn. He's the guy who installed the electric-eye system at Kahn's place. This creep's got so many angles he doesn't know whether he's coming or going. But he really knows his stuff."

"If he works for Kahn, he's not gonna work for me.

After all, Marsha runs the prostitution for Ricca and Kahn. Merkle knows that. And besides, he knows me, too. He did some stuff for the Vice Squad when I was down there. We didn't get along too well."

"Listen, Ernie. This creep is really afraid of Kahn. If Kahn knew he did work for the police he'd blow his brains out. Remind Merkle of that little fact."

And that had been that. Now, Tucker was on his way to Merkle's shop on Santa Monica Boulevard. The traffic was heavy and slow this time of the morning and it annoyed him more than usual. The smog was already cutting out the sun and he could feel it in his nasal passages. His eyes were beginning to smart. He found Merkle's place in a deteriorating section of Santa Monica Boulevard and brought his three-year-old Ford to a slow stop. The sign painted on the plate glass window said *Merkle's Electronics*. It was a small shop, dirty and cluttered with dozens of radios and television sets in various stages of repair. Tucker walked in and stopped before a counter.

The place seemed empty. A radio was playing and he could hear a disk jockey expounding on the merits of a particular brand of shortening. Tucker rapped on the counter a couple of times, then walked around it to the back of the shop.

There was a long workbench with tools scattered all over it. Tucker glanced at the tools, then walked across to the other side of the room to a heavy wooden door. There was a padlock on the door, one of those huge affairs that worked on a three-combination system. To Tucker's suspicious eye, the heavy lock gained immediate importance and he leaned against the door, listening. He didn't hear anything at first, then he heard it, a muffled sound, like someone talking into a microphone. He couldn't make out the words, but he knew it was a man's voice. The sound seemed to fade in and out, like whoever was talking kept walking away from the mike.

Then, from across the room, Tucker heard the sound of a toilet being flushed and he stepped away from the door and waited. Merkle came into the room, pulling at his suspenders, and Tucker spoke up before the little man saw him. Merkle gave a start, his small mouth popping open in surprise.

"What in hell," he cried. "You shouldn't be back here." Then he recognized Tucker and tried to smile. "Oh, it's you, Sergeant. What are you doing here?"

"I'd like to talk over a little business with you," Tucker said.

"Well, hell, I'm in a hurry right now. Gotta make a call." He hurried to the workbench and started picking up tools and placing them in a heavy leather toolcase.

"This won't take long," Tucker said, thinking about the peculiar sound behind the heavy locked door.

"I don't really have the time. See me tomorrow."

"Okay," Tucker said, and started toward the front of the shop.

"What was it?" Merkle asked.

"It'll keep," Tucker said, as he went out the front door.

Marty Kahn's Bel Air estate was just about par for the swanky neighborhood. There was the usual huge house with too many rooms and lots of big fat brass doorknobs. And there was the also usual tiled swimming pool and flagstone patio with all the tropical plants and palm trees planted full grown to give the *nouveau riche*, impatient owner a sense of belonging and permanency. And as always there was a fantastic panoramic view of the sprawling city below, a city lying at Marty Kahn's feet.

Kahn was one of the more recent residents in Bel Air. It had taken him ten years of fighting and stealing and slugging to worm his way up that mountain stronghold. Two months previous, in celebration of the grand opening, he had led a Cadillac motorcade of hoods and bookies up the steep, narrow, twisting Bel Air road and properly christened the joint with a party that had lasted for three days.

The newspapers had carried the story. Radio and television commentators described the great house in minute detail. One enterprising television sob sister took her viewers on a guided tour, trotting and gushing at Marty's side as he freely and expansively expounded on the origin and price of everything.

Marty Kahn was proud of his mansion. Proud that he, the son of a punch-drunk club fighter, had risen from the ghettos of Brooklyn Avenue, east of the Los Angeles River, to the dizzy heights of aristocratic Bel Air in West Los Angeles. He had made the long, hazardous journey across town from east to west, from poverty to riches, from smog to clean mountain air, from crime to power and more and bigger crimes.

This was much more than just a house to Marty Kahn. It was a showplace, a shrine erected to his enterprising genius. It was proof that Marty Kahn had made the big time and in a big way. Who could deny or even argue against this show of evidence. Who could doubt that Marty Kahn was big and important and smart. Here stood a majestic structure of steel and tile and brick and glass, low and long with sweeping lines and curves; and all of it circled by a six-foot-high white brick fence that enclosed and protected, by an electric-eye system, a whole acre of the highest-priced real estate this side of Manhattan.

But this morning, two months after the grand opening, Marty Kahn was not happy. His thoughts had strayed far from the luxury and comfort of his demesne. Something was awry within the manor. The juice had lost its magic.

Protection was suddenly impossible to buy. Eastern interests were challenging his power. The serfs were agitating. Rebellion seemed imminent. And Marty Kahn, his feudal lordship himself, was getting nervous. Real nervous.

He sat at a glass-topped table on the patio reading the morning newspaper, ready to start on his sixth cup of coffee, when Marie joined him. She was dressed in a white terry robe, her deeply tanned face without make-up except for plenty of coral lipstick. He had finished reading the headline story, and had gone twice over the open letter he had submitted to the newspapers the day before, and which was now printed on an inside page of the paper.

"Jesus H. Christ," he said, without looking up. "Them stupid papers can't even print a letter without getting wise. Listen to this goddam headline: 'Kahn begs neighbors for right to live and let live.'

"Where the hell did they get that 'beg' crap. Marty Kahn begs nobody. All I do is write an open letter to my neighbors and the bastards have to be cute. Listen to this garbage," he said, gulping down some coffee, a little of it trickling down his chin.

Marie had started eating her grapefruit, her face puckering up every time she took a bite. "Yeah," she said, recovering long enough from a pucker to assume a look of interest. "What'd it say?"

Marty brought the paper up close to his face and started to read.

"Marty Kahn, Bel Air's bad boy, who was bombed last Saturday, appealed yesterday to his Bel Air neighbors for a chance to live peacefully among them.

"His plea was contained in a mimeographed open letter sent special delivery to the shocked residents unfortunate enough to live within firing range of Kahn's fortress.

"The letter came as an answer by Kahn to the demand made Monday by a group of residents to the district's councilman, John Brody Aston, that immediate steps be taken to rid the neighborhood of its chief nuisance, namely Marty Kahn.

"'Yeah, Marty wrote it, all right,' the little mobster's girl friend, Marie, told a reporter. 'Marty don't like for people to be mad at him. It makes him nervous.'"

Marie was silent.

"God damn it," Marty shouted. "Why don't you keep your stupid trap shut."

"Goodness, you don't have to shout like that. I'm not deaf, you know. I can hear you perfectly good."

"God damn it," Marty shouted again.

"Don't get yourself worked up now," she cautioned.

Marty slammed the newspaper against the table, upsetting a platter of toast.

"Now look what you've done," Marie cried.

"Shut up," Kahn shouted. "So help me, the next time you open your stupid yap, I'm gonna drown you in that goddam pool."

"Now, Marty," she said, her voice sweet and sugary. "You're not mad at your little playmate, are you?"

Marty glared at her, exasperated to the point of helplessness.

"Read the letter again, Marty, I like the sound of it. All those big words. Makes you sound important. Boy, that Barker is sure a smart cookie."

"What do you mean? I wrote that goddam letter. He helped here and there, but I wrote it."

"Read it," she said. "It sounds real fancy."

Marty picked up the paper and started to read.

"An Open Letter to My Neighbors:

"On Saturday morning some mad fiends threw a bomb in my front yard. This outrage created a great threat to my friends and neighbors and has deprived me of the security and sanctuary of my home. As grievous as this act was, it did not injure me as much as the action of some of my neighbors in trying to remove me from this charming community.

"This action came as a great shock to me. Instead of receiving the consideration and consolation and sympathy that I so needed at that time from my neighbors, I was requested to leave, leave like a thief in the night.

"It is difficult for me to understand why these neighbors, whom I have never molested in any way, would want to hurt me. They must be aware that despite much adverse newspaper publicity, not one single iota of proof can be shown to justify the kind of savagery that occurred last Saturday morning.

"Everyone knows that I have done nothing in self-defense so as not to endanger my neighbors in any way. In fact, I have even sent lifelong friends away to avoid wrong and unsavory appearances.

"Please, neighbors, let's stop kidding ourselves. Clear-thinking people know that my position has been misrepresented by crackpot writers interested more in sensationalism than in the truth, because the truth would be dull and ordinary. I live quietly in almost semiretirement. So in the future don't believe everything you read.

"Let me state it again, once and for all. I am not a mobster, a gunman, or a thug. I am merely a businessman who owns a number of legitimate businesses, and sometimes likes to make a bet or two. No more, no less.

"I still have faith in my neighbors. I have faith that most of my neighbors are decent, levelheaded people with tolerance in their heart for an underdog. And I know they won't give those mad fiends who lit that bomb the satisfaction of seeing me leave the home I have come to love so much. I don't think anyone in this beautiful community really wants to hurt me.

"Very truly, your friendly neighbor, Marty Kahn."

"Beautiful," Marie said, as Marty finished reading the letter. "It really grabs me, especially that part about love in their hearts for the underdog."

"An underdog," he corrected. "The doctor wanted me to cut that part out. Hell, them lawyers are all the same. Big legal words that don't mean nothing to the average person. Take me, now, I didn't go to no law school. I didn't even go to high school, but I dictate business letters every day. I do business with college guys all the time. And when I talk, they listen. Christ, I wouldn't give a penny for that college crap. As my punchy old man used to say, they pickle your brain in them colleges."

He stood up and stretched, breaking into a fast boxing shuffle, his heavy shoulders and arms moving like well-oiled pistons. He wore only a pair of swimming trunks, and his dark chest and back were almost completely covered with black, wiry hair. His soft belly spilled over the tight waist of the trunks, shaking as he danced around shadow-boxing. Sitting down it became a cascading mass of flabby rolls. Marty Kahn was getting soft. Real soft.

Marie picked up a glass of buttermilk and closed her eyes as it went down her throat.

"For Christ sakes," Marty called to her, sending a couple of fast jabs in her direction. "Why drink the stuff if you hate it?"

"It's good for you," she said, downing the rest of it. "They say it's very healthy."

"Healthy! Christ, you're already as healthy as a pig."

"I'm not, either," she whined. She had started to remove the pearl-pink polish from her nails with the acetone remover, and her usually smooth forehead was creased in concentration.

"Not here," Marty shouted, pointing at the acetone.

"Take that stinking crap out of here. And tell Little Abner to get his fat ass over here pronto."

She stuck out her tongue at him as soon as he spun around, drilling a right hook into some imaginary face. She picked up her bottles of nail polish and polish remover and hurried into the house, her usually undulating hips swinging indignantly.

Little Abner wasn't exactly little. He stood six-six in his stocking feet and weighed over two hundred and sixty-five pounds. His neck was as big as Marie's waist, and he towered an even foot over Marty. He came out of the house now, running in usual lumbering gait, his vapid face almost worried.

"Yeah, Marty," he called, in a dry, hoarse voice. "Didja call me?"

"Com'on," Marty said, impatiently. "Let's go. I wanna get some exercise before the doctor gets here."

Little Abner hurried forward, his barren face trying as usual to assume an air of interest. But it was hopeless. Little Abner had no control over his facial expressions.

Marty feinted with a right and swung a sharp left hook into Little Abner's stomach, then followed quickly with a fast one-two punch. Little Abner stepped back too hurriedly and stumbled. Marty was all over him, his heavy fists pounding the giant right into the ground. Little Abner was sitting down, his big arms raised to protect his face. Marty laughed and danced back.

"Com'on, robot," he laughed. "Get off your fat ass and fight."

Slowly, cautiously, Little Abner stood up, ready at any moment to drop again if Marty came at him.

"Awe, Marty. I don't wanta fight. I've got a belly ache. I think I'm constipated."

"Oh, loving Jesus," Marty cried, his dark pudgy face red with excitement. "The robot is constipated. That's one for the book. Holy Christ! I've gotta tell that one to the doctor."

"Can I go now, Marty?" Little Abner asked. "I wanta wash the car down this morning. Needs a real cleaning."

"I don't know why," Marty said. "It hasn't been out of here in two weeks. And the way things look right now, it probably won't for the next two weeks. Jesus, those sons a bitches are getting on my goddam nerves."

"Hey, Marty, when are we gonna get those punks?"

"We'll get 'em, all right," he said, not quite sure whom he meant. "Don't worry about that. But we've got to wait for the right time. Too much heat right now. Christ! The fuzz would have to get Joe on a goddam murder rap. Everything happens to me. There's no goddam justice left for me."

"We'll get 'em," Little Abner said, edging toward the house.

"Aw, go wash the goddam car," Marty said, suddenly tired of the subject and of Little Abner.

9.

When Bryce Barker arrived at the Bel Air estate, Marty was in the pool. Barker waved to him and sat down at the glass-topped table. He was tired. It had been a rough night and it looked like an even rougher day ahead.

He was used to getting only four or five hours of sleep, but last night he hadn't had any sleep at all. The cops had given him the run-around all night until finally he had felt foolish and impotent. By the time he had arranged a meeting with Ricca and Doto, daylight had been breaking over the sleeping city. Then the writ of habeas corpus hadn't done any good, either. It wasn't returnable for another four days. When finally he got back to his apartment, he was exhausted. He shaved, showered and changed clothes. He put away half a dozen drinks while puzzling over the frustrating aspects of the case, then went out and had a thick steak for breakfast.

He felt a little better then, but still tired. The muscles behind his eyes ached and burned, but his head felt clearer and strangely sharp. He watched Marty wallowing in the pool, diving under the water, then shooting out, his whole torso exposed and glistening, blowing water like a porpoise, then going under again, only to repeat the whole process.

Marty, he thought, was working out his frustration, beating himself into a physical stupor. Bryce was pleased. He knew from past experience that the exercise would calm him down, relax him a little, at least for a while. He must have been really high this morning, Bryce thought, smiling ruefully. God, when is he going to flip over that thin dividing line for good? That's all I need right now. Marty Kahn in a state of acute mania. Then we'll really be in a bind. What a goddam unholy mess this whole stinking operation is becoming. Two months ago Marty was king, sitting on top of the world. And then everything went crazy. Without the slightest warning, Marty Kahn was on the outside looking in, all the protection money down the drain, every important contact gone. The word had gone out and Kahn's name had become taboo. A dirty word.

Bryce had his suspicions. For one thing, the big boy in Sacramento had fallen out of favor with the powers that be. There were a lot of rumbles, too, about the mafia moving in, bringing in their kind of organized crime. And Marty Kahn was in the way.

That was why it was so important to get Ricca and Doto out of jail. Marty would need them when the showdown came, and from the appearance of things, it would come soon. Too damn soon.

Then Bryce remembered Alan Avery, glanced again at the picture on the front page of the newspaper lying on the table. And he remembered a tall, lanky kid of sixteen with a big smile and quiet easy manners. A kid who had been a friend. A good friend.

He leaned forward and looked closely at the picture. There wasn't any smile on the face now. The face looked grim and older. And he wondered what would happen to Alan when Ricca got out. Something would have to be done to protect Alan.

When Barker looked up from the newspaper, Marty was standing next to him, vigorously rubbing his thick, hairy body with a huge turkish towel. Barker instantly recognized the wild and unpredictable look in Marty's eyes, and as always it made him feel like walking on tiptoe. Nothing should be done to upset that delicate balance wheel now clicking away in that complex brain.

"What's all this crap in the paper about Joe? Why ain't he out like I told you? God damn it, you know I need him. Listen, you better stop screwing around and get me some action. Man, I want action and I want it now. Get it!"

"Take it easy, Marty," Bryce cautioned, his voice even and smooth. He was using his courtroom voice now, trying to placate his highly agitated boss. It was the same kind of voice the psychiatrist used in a couch session. "You know as well as I do there's no bail on a murder charge."

"Don't crap me, Doctor. Where's the goddam corpus delectus. They can't hold Joe without a stiff. Christ, you oughtta know that. You're a goddam lawyer, ain't you?"

"Corpus delicti," Barker corrected.

"Delectus, delecti, who gives a damn. The fact is Joe is in the can and I want him out. Now!"

"Just a minute," Barker said. "To use your own words, corpus delicti doesn't refer to the corpse itself. It actually refers to the substance of a crime: that is, to the substantial fact that a crime has been committed, in this instance, murder. The witness says murder was committed. The police found blood at the scene just as described by the witness. They then picked up the owner of the car identified by the witness, plus plenty of blood in the car, plus the fact that the suspects are habitual criminals. And don't forget, Danchik is missing. That, in essence, is the corpus delicti."

"Don't con me with all that hokus-pokus crap. They ain't got no stiff and unless they find one damn quick, they ain't got no case. Christ, I've been in this business long enough to know that. So don't con me, Doctor. I don't like it." He threw down the towel and glared at Barker, his eyes flashing with anger.

"Sit down and let's talk this over calmly."

"And don't tell me what to do," Kahn shouted, sitting down.

"I could use a cup of coffee," Barker said. "I've been up all night. On second thought, make it a double Scotch and soda."

"Hey, Lenora," Marty called, and a huge Mexican woman came trotting out to the patio.

"Yes, sir, yes, sir," she chanted, her fat face open in a wide smile. "Something for your friend?"

"Yeah," Marty said. "Bring us some coffee."

Marty waited for the woman to leave and then burst out laughing.

"Forgot to tell you," he said, laughing till the tears flooded his eyes. "The robot is constipated." And he slapped the table so hard that Barker thought the glass top would shatter.

"Forget about that drink," he said. "Too early, and you

drink too damn much, anyway. I don't like for my guys to drink too much. It ain't good for my business." He was serious again, the change having taken place in a split second. "Did you see what them wise reporters did to that letter of mine. Begs! Jesus, how do you like that. Marty Kahn begs nobody. Ever. Everything I got I took. And I wasn't begging. I took what I wanted because I was smarter and stronger. And that's no crap. I was in the goddam ring when I was fourteen, fighting professional. Got a lousy two bucks per. How about Joe? What are you gonna do?"

The Mexican servant brought the coffee and Marty laughed when she placed the cup in front of Barker.

"How about it, Lenora? Coffee strong enough for him, heh?"

She laughed, displaying red, toothless gums. "Yes, sir, plenty strong."

"Where's Jesus?" Kahn asked, giving the Mexican name an American pronunciation.

She laughed again. "Watering the flowers," she said, referring to her eighteen-year-old son, a tall, dark, curly-haired boy who worked as houseboy in the Kahn household.

"There, see," Kahn laughed, slapping the table, rocking the coffee cups on their saucers. "Jesus is out there watering my plants. You can't be much bigger than that."

Barker forced a smile and took a sip of coffee. "You're big, all right," he said.

"Something's gotta be done about that bum Avery."

"Let's not rush into anything until we know the full score."

"Yeah. Well, that bum better change his mind goddam quick. That's all I got to tell you."

"Hell, Marty, we've got enough trouble right now without looking for more."

"Don't you worry about that. I can handle it."

"This is different. There's no connections now. We have to take it easy for a while."

"How about Joe? You think he's gonna take it easy?"

"To hell with Joe. Let him take care of himself."

Kahn stared at Barker, his pudgy face slowly turning red with rage. "You better not talk like that, Doctor. It ain't healthy. Not a goddam bit."

Barker raised the coffee cup to his lips and took a sip, his gray eyes studying Marty over the rim of the cup, his hands trembling with emotion. He hated Kahn more at this moment than he could possibly endure. And deep down, buried in the dark recesses of his repressed mind, he knew he hated Kahn because of what he saw of himself. Bryce Barker sitting beside a swimming pool, drinking coffee with a crude barbarian. Bryce Barker, the fast-talking gangster mouthpiece. Bryce Barker the sycophant, the prostitute, the lush.

What had happened to the boy with the dream he had once shared with Alan Avery. The dream with a real beginning and the now so pathetic ending. He longed for that dream until he could feel it inside of him, twisting and turning.

"Maybe you better get yourself another lawyer," he said, the anger trembling through him like a horrible sickness.

"Shut up," Kahn shouted. "Don't get smart with me. I'm not paying you a hundred grand a year for a lot of wise talk. Joe's my boy and we're gonna do all we can to spring him. Even if I have to hit that goddam teacher myself."

Barker fought for self-control. It was important that he stay calm if he were to help Alan. And helping Alan was suddenly the most important thing in the world to him. This was the only way he could redeem himself for himself.

This was salvation. And he wanted it so badly that it made him feel reckless enough to jeopardize his own safety. And that was breaking the number-one rule governing Barker's world.

He forced a smile, making his voice soft and even again, in the courtroom manner. "Let me talk to the teacher, Marty. Maybe there's a solution."

Marty laughed. "God damn it! That's more like the old doctor."

Suddenly he jumped up and whistled, a low suggestive wolf call, clapping his hands loudly together. Barker turned and saw Marie walking toward the swimming pool, her brown body glistening in the bright sunlight, her wide hips swaying the small patch of white cloth stretched tight across her full round buttocks in a slow, inviting tempo, her full breasts held loosely by an even smaller wisp of white cloth, the whole front assembly bouncing recklessly with every step of her high heels on the flagstone walk, struggling for release.

"Man," Marty cried hoarsely. "That's a woman!"

"Yes," Bryce agreed. "There's no doubt of that."

"What would you do with something like that, Doctor?" Kahn laughed, slapping Bryce on the shoulder.

"Oh, I don't know," Barker said. "I'd probably think of something."

Marty guffawed and slapped again. "Man, that really grabs me. Think of something. You're goddam right you'd think of something. Man, that kind of meat's got to be cared for. You got to nourish it. Keep it hot in the winter and cool in the summer like the old song says. Get it?"

"Oh, sure," Bruce said. "Mink in the winter and bikinis in the summer. I follow you, all right."

"That's no goddam lie," Marty said, his eyes fixed on Marie. She was sitting down on a huge foam-rubber pad, rubbing suntan lotion on her thighs. She looked up and smiled and Marty whistled again.

Barker knew that Marty had lost all interest in the conversation. His thoughts were now on Marie. And what he had on his mind at the moment had nothing to do with Joe Ricca or Alan Avery. Like most manic-depressives, Marty had a very low boiling point. And Marie kept it up there boiling most of the time. The urge came quick and often, and like everything else with the manic, it had to be immediately gratified.

Marie finished with the lotion and turned over on her stomach, her body arched back, straining as her hands reached to undo the knot on the brief halter. She lay facing the two men and for a brief moment, when the halter came undone, the huge breasts were completely exposed, then she quickly came forward, resting her weight on them, burying them into the softness of the foam rubber pad.

"Well," Marty said, his eyes riveted on Marie. "Go talk to the bum. And you tell him we're not gonna play around, either. I want action and I want it now. Today!"

"I'll do my best. Now how about the conspiracy case? You know this Bruckner is out for a payoff, and I don't think it'd take too much. The case is coming up to trial in about a week. I think we can make it without Bruckner's help, but it would be quicker and safer with a payoff."

"That can wait," Marty said, standing up and patting his loose belly. "Man, that was the craziest yet. Those stupid bums going down a dead-end street. Christ, how can you figure creeps like that. A goddam dead-end street." His hands held his shaking head....

Marty Kahn had plenty of reasons to hold his head when he thought of the Bruckner case. Here was something so stupid that it was almost unbelievable. It had actually been the beginning of all his troubles. Not that Bruckner had anything to do with the events that followed, but Kahn had lost seven top hoodlums in one mad, stupid caper. It had left the way open for the syndicate to move in without too much opposition. It had been done quietly, without any real show of force or any showdown. Marty, himself, wasn't even sure of what was going on. At first, he thought it was some local hoods trying to muscle in on him. But that was hard to believe, especially for Marty Kahn. No one in Los Angeles, he was sure, could be so foolish as to try such a dumb trick.

Then, slowly, the word leaked out and Marty was one of the first to hear it. The mafia was moving in. The syndicate was coming to the West Coast. That was all he knew, and now he waited for someone from the mafia to approach him, waited for the showdown that would inevitably come.

And he had the Bruckner case to thank for all that misery. One lousy butcher, and one little old lady without a home. Kahn had read about it in the papers. A Miss Lucy Meyers had been sued by an Alfred Bruckner for money owed to him for the purchase of meat over a period of two years. Miss Meyers owed the said Bruckner two hundred and forty-one dollars, and Bruckner obtained a judgment, then later bought Miss Meyers's house at a sheriff's auction for three hundred and ten dollars. The house was valued at sixty-five hundred.

The case had greatly irritated Kahn and he had called on Bruckner, demanding that the butcher return the property to Miss Meyers. Bruckner, a huge man with a thick German accent, had picked up an ugly carving knife and had chased Marty from his shop. Marty brooded about the incident for two days, then sent a carload of seven hoods down to teach Bruckner a lesson. They arrived at the butcher shop armed with guns, knives, tire irons and lead pipes, and one eccentric hood carried a riding crop. In less than four minutes they fractured Bruckner's skull

in three places, broke both his arms, five ribs and one ankle, and inflicted countless cuts and contusions. Bruckner
was unconscious for over forty-eight hours, and he was
still in the hospital. After taking care of Bruckner, the
hoods ran out of the shop and leaped into the big Cadillac
parked in the front with the motor running, made a wild
U-turn and sped down a dead-end street just as a patrol
car was leisurely cruising by.

The patrol car gave chase with full siren and red light
blinking. Lead pipes, guns, tire irons, knives and one
riding crop flew out of the windows of the speeding Cadillac. Then it was all over. The Cadillac came to a shrieking
halt before an eight-foot stone wall. The officers lined up
the hoods and waited for the assistance of three patrol
cars which arrived on the scene in less than five minutes.

The discarded articles were retrieved from nearby lawns
and the men were taken in for booking.

Kahn heard of the arrest and put his connections to
work. The seven hoodlums were immediately released
without being booked and their weapons returned to
them. There was only one kicker to the whole thing, and
it turned it into a political football. One of the neighbors
at the scene of the arrest took a picture of the hoods with
their hands above their heads and sent it to a local newspaper.

Things began to happen. The hoods were re-arrested,
and Kahn found himself right in the middle of it. The
mayor made a statement to the effect that anyone protecting hoodlums in the city of Los Angeles would be
cleared out of the police department. "It seems," His
Honor said, "there are rotten apples in the barrel."

Bail was set at seventy-five thousand for each of the
seven hoods, and one hundred thousand for Kahn, making
a total of six hundred and twenty-five thousand dollars.
Kahn raised the hundred thousand for himself and left

the seven hoodlums in jail.

"I still think we could approach Bruckner," Bryce said. "This fellow has a great passion for money. I think a little of it could go a long way."

"Screw that. I'm not giving that bum one lousy red cent. We're gonna beat that rap. The sympathy of the people is with us."

"I hope the judge agrees with you."

"What the hell do you mean you hope so? For Christ sakes, Doctor, don't you know?"

"It's a little more complicated than you seem to think."

"Ah, shove it," Marty said, glancing at Marie. "I've got more important things on my mind right now. You go see that bum. And listen, I'm not gonna foots around with him. Remember that."

Barker stood up and tried to smile but he couldn't. He just looked at the pudgy little man, then turned around and hurried out.

"Don't forget," Kahn yelled. "I want action. Now!" But Barker had already disappeared through the sliding glass door leading into the house.

Kahn turned and walked toward Marie, grinning.

"You little bitch," he said, placing a bare foot on her warm buttocks. "You trying to get the doctor all hot and bothered?"

"What do you mean?" she asked, turning her head around to look up at him, her eyes narrowed against the brilliant sun.

"You know goddam well what I mean. Showing off your tits like that." And he laughed, pressing down hard with his foot, slowly rotating her firm, round buttocks.

She smiled a slow suggestive smile that curved her red lips slowly over her white teeth. "No one asked you guys to watch."

"Stand up," he said, removing his foot.

"What for?"

"Stand up!"

"I'm comfortable."

"God damn it, stand up!"

She reached back to tie the thin strap of white cloth and his foot came up and quickly roiled her over. "Never mind that thing," he said.

She looked down at the whiteness of her untanned breasts and saw the huge foot come up and cover her left breast.

"Marty!" she screamed, rolling over and jumping up to her feet.

"Take the bottom off," he said, his dark eyes now cloudy with desire.

"No, Marty. What if somebody came out?"

"Take it off," he shouted.

"Jeez," she said, looking back toward the house, her fingers nervously working at the knots holding the small patch of white cloth to her hips. "I feel foolish."

Marty stepped forward and quickly ripped the cloth off, the violence almost knocking her down. She stood naked in the bright sunlight, her tan body marked by a thin bone-white stripe across her full breasts and a small bone-white triangle that reached halfway up to her navel.

"Okay," he said, his eyes devouring her naked body. "Run around the pool."

"Oh, Marty, not that. It makes me feel so foolish."

"Go on, run."

"Damn," she said, stamping her foot, her whole body responding to the sudden shock.

"Run," he said, taking a step toward her. She started running, slowly at first, awkwardly; then she ran a little faster, her body shaking, fascinating Marty as he stood watching her, his dark eyes taking in every part of her vibrating anatomy.

"Faster," he called, when she had reached the other side of the pool. And she ran faster, in that typically feminine way, her full breasts bouncing almost in a circular motion, her buttocks jiggling up and down. She completed the turn around the pool and stopped before him breathing hard, her red mouth open, hungrily gulping air.

"Come here," he said, his voice hoarse and trembling. And she came to him and he pulled her close against him, pressing his fat lips roughly against hers, and she felt his big, soft hand slide up her waist and over her breasts, stopping over one of them, and then she felt the hardness of him against her, and she tried to pull away, not wanting it to happen there in the bright sunlight.

He released her and then pulled her back, grinning at her, the passion sweeping through him like wild fire. "Get into the pool," he said, his voice low and hoarse. "Go on!"

"Oh, Marty, not now. Tonight. Okay? We'll do it tonight when nobody's around."

"Jump in," he said, starting to peel off his trunks.

She ran then and dove into the pool, the cool water pure and clean against her hot body. She shot up to the surface, her legs kicking powerfully, her hands pushing the matted hair back from her face. She opened her eyes and saw Marty standing at the edge of the pool, naked, leering down at her, poised for a dive.

"Float on your back," he called. "Move your legs over this way. I'll dive between them."

She rolled onto her back, her arms and legs fluttering lightly, keeping her afloat.

"Here I come," he called, and dove, his dark, hairy body cutting the water in front of her. She struggled to stay afloat, the water swirling about her, then she felt his arm around her waist, pulling her under, turning her around slowly as they drifted to the bottom of the pool.

10.

Don Merkle visited the Kahn estate every Friday morning, to check the electric-eye system. It was set up so that whenever anyone penetrated the electric eye, a signal bell would ring throughout the house. On such occasions, Marty would flip a switch and the entire grounds would be lighted up by powerful floods. Merkle also checked for hidden bugs and taps. He checked, that is, for any hidden taps and bugs that weren't his own.

In the past ten years, Merkle had tapped and bugged hundreds of homes, apartments, offices and public places. Now, he had committed himself to the most daring of all his adventures—bugging the palatial home of Marty Kahn.

Merkle understood the risk of such an enterprise, but he also understood the reward. Important names had come into his possession, and these names had disclosed important facts, facts worth thousands in extortion. In the two months that Merkle had been listening to the private business of Marty Kahn, he had learned much of the operation, knew about bookie drops, houses of prostitution, and had compiled a long list of crooked cops and politicians.

Merkle was a little man with a big ambition. Some day he wanted to own a home like Marty Kahn's. He wanted to live in Bel Air and belong to the Bel Air Country Club and play golf with the movie stars. He wanted a swimming pool and a couple of Cadillacs, and most of all, he wanted a blonde sex machine like that Marie, something to keep him young in his old age. Money, lots of money, he was sure, would buy all of that.

He drove up in his small pickup truck and stopped before the heavy wrought-iron gates. He could see Little

Abner bending over the grille of the Cadillac, polishing the chrome, and he hit the horn with the palm of his hand. Little Abner stood up and slowly came forward to open the gate.

"Getting your exercise, I see," Merkle shouted, as he drove by the huge man. He brought the truck to a stop a little way past the Caddy and jumped out of the truck. Little Abner lumbered up to him, his heavy face expressionless.

"Smell this air," Merkle said, standing on tiptoe as he took a heavy draught of air into his lungs. "Man, how I love this clean-smelling mountain air. Reminds me of my kid days on the farm. Except on the farm there was always piles of manure around to crap up the good smell. But sometimes in the morning, when the wind was blowing right, it smelled just like this."

Little Abner nodded his big head in agreement. "Yeah. Smells good. Me, I was brought up in the city. Right there on the East Side, with Marty."

"I know what it smells like over there," Merkle said, sliding a heavy leather toolcase from the back of the truck. "Where's the boss this morning?"

"Out on the patio," Little Abner said. "But don't go there. He don't want nobody bothering him."

"Okay," Merkle said, and he started walking back to the gate, the heavy bag pulling him sideways. He now would have to walk around the entire fence, checking all the terminals. Then he would go into the house and check the control board. Maybe if he had a chance he would put in another bug. This time in the bedroom. Man, that one would be just for kicks. He sure would like to hear what went on in there. Might be real exciting. Well, he'd have to wait and see how things were first. He started whistling, not even aware of the heavy bag any more.

Little Abner watched Merkle walk toward the fence,

his brain struggling with the problem of making a decision. Should he tell Marty that Merkle was here? Merkle was now walking along the fence and would soon come to a full view of the pool. Little Abner had seen Marie running naked around the pool, and he knew that now they were lying, still naked, on the foam rubber mat. He hated to go out there when they were like that, but maybe it was better for him to see them than Merkle.

He could stand in the doorway and call to him. Maybe that would be best. He watched as Merkle stopped at the second terminal and opened up his leather toolcase. Three more terminals and he would have a full view of the pool. Little Abner dropped the polishing cloth and hurried toward the house. He would have to take his chances.

Marie was lying on her stomach, while Marty rubbed suntan lotion on the patches of white flesh. She giggled a little as his hand moved across her buttocks, hesitating a moment at the base of her spine, and then quickly moving downward.

"No, Marty," she cried, flipping herself on her back just as Little Abner called from the doorway.

"Oh, my God!" she cried, rolling onto her stomach again, trying to cover her exposed buttocks with her hands. Marty looked up and saw Little Abner, his head down, his eyes fixed on his big feet.

"Come here," Marty said, grinning at Little Abner's embarrassed approach.

"Merkle's here," Little Abner mumbled, his eyes looking up at the blue sky now that he stood towering over Marty. "He's checking the fence."

"I've got to get out of here," Marie said. "I don't want that little creep peeking at me."

"Relax," Marty said, grinning up at Little Abner, who still stood gazing up at the sky. "I hope when you get yourself a mistress, Little Abner, she's as modest as Marie.

This little girl don't like to show her ass in public."

Little Abner just stood gazing at the sky, unable to think of an appropriate answer. "God damn it, look at me when I talk to you," Marty shouted. Slowly, Little Abner looked down, his eyes uncontrollably shifting to Marie.

Marty laughed and slapped Marie across the buttocks. Little Abner saw the red finger marks on the white flesh and quickly looked skyward again.

"For goodness sakes," Marie cried. "Can't you send him away."

"Okay, okay," Marty said, waving Little Abner away with a toss of his head, and laughed as the huge man hurried away in his lumbering gait.

As soon as Little Abner disappeared into the house Marie sat up and reached for the white halter. Marty watched her as she tied it on, then as she tried to stand up he reached over and pinched her high inside the thigh. She screamed and jumped back, her red lips pulled back over her white teeth.

"You've gotta stop that. It's dangerous."

"Come here," he said.

"No!"

"Come here."

"No. Haven't you had enough?"

"Come here!"

Quickly she reached down and picked up the other piece of white cloth and ran for the house, holding the cloth in front of her, and all the time hearing Marty's loud laugh behind her.

After she had disappeared inside the house, Marty stood up and leisurely walked into the house, stopping to bow arrogantly before the Mexican maid, who was arranging flowers in the living room. He looked at her, taking pleasure in her embarrassment.

"God damn it," he said. "This place stinks. Do something. Clean up. Vacuum. Get that goddam stink out." And then proudly walked out before the woman could answer.

He showered and shaved. Then, dressed in slacks, Hawaiian sport shirt and sandals, he went back out to the patio to wait for Merkle.

He felt tired, without interest or purpose. Everything was going sour. After all these years of hard work, it just wasn't fair. It confused him. And Marty Kahn hadn't felt confused in a long time.

Somewhere in the back of his mind, feebly struggling for expression, was a feeling of failure, and he tried to fight it, drive the thought back where it came from, but he couldn't gather enough energy to force it back. Everything was lousy. And it was all his fault. He was a failure. And with the thought came that familiar hollowness in the pit of his stomach, slowly spreading until the feeling seemed to press against his heart, making him weak and nauseous. He never could understand the emptiness. Sometimes he would wake up in the morning and it would be there, gnawing at his insides like a malignant growth. Then he would mope around all day, his thoughts completely introverted, feeling sad and sorry for himself.

This feeling became so all-encompassing at times that he had to go to bed, where he could be completely alone with his thoughts. And sometimes on those days, he became ill, seriously ill, and the doctor would come and give him a strong sedative and soon Marty would float off into a deep, dreamless sleep, Other times, though, he didn't want the doctor. On those days he enjoyed playing a game with that devouring emptiness. He fed it. Fed it with what it wanted most of all: abuse. And he would lie in the bed and think up all kinds of vile and ugly names to call himself, deriving a great masochistic pleasure in shocking the emptiness. Sometimes, to really shock that horrible lurking beast, he would wish for death, tell himself that he had it coming to him. That he was vile and bad and wasn't fit to live. Then the emptiness would change into a black, blinding fear that shot the emptiness all through his body like a poison, pitching him deeper into the depression.

Usually the depression didn't last more than a day, and often not more than an hour or two. Immediately after the depression, he would become highly exhilarated as a boundless energy surged through him, making him unusually gay and talkative. Marie never really understood these moods and dismissed the whole thing with a shrug and a few words. Marty was "in the dumps" or having his "ups." She never questioned the strangeness of it. To her it was just Marty's way. And who was she to question the ways of a man so successful....

It took Merkle a little over forty minutes to check the entire fence and the control board. Everything was in good working order. He wondered whether he should try to place the bug in Marty's bedroom. He tried to think of some logical excuse he could use if discovered, but he couldn't think of any except the usual one that he was checking to see if any bugs had been planted. It would mean that he would have to cut his way into the wall, preferably just behind the bed, and that would be damn hard to explain, especially if he were caught while cutting into it.

He picked up his bag and walked out of the den, across the living room and down to the end of a long hallway. He stopped before the closed door to Marty's bedroom. Slowly, he turned the knob and eased himself into the room. The venetian blinds were down and he had to wait a moment for his eyes to adjust to the partially darkened room. He stood by the door, his eyes slowly moving across the large room. Suddenly, he caught his breath and pressed his small body against the closed door. Marie was lying on the bed, stark naked, and a tall, dark man was standing by the bed, stroking the inside of her leg. Merkle squinted his eyes and quickly recognized Jesus, the Mexican houseboy. Marie just lay there, her eyes closed, whimpering softly.

Holding his breath, Merkle slowly opened the door and slipped out into the hallway without making a sound. He leaned against the wall and wiped his brow with the back of his hand. "Christ," he whispered softly. "Jesus H. Christ!"

He hurried out of the patio and saw Marty sitting in a canvas chair by the pool.

"Hi," he called, waving his hand in greeting.

Marty slowly looked up, frowned, then looked down again at his folded hands.

"Everything okay," Merkle said, putting the heavy toolcase down and sitting next to Marty.

"What?" Marty asked, frowning again.

"I've just checked the system. All okay."

"Oh," Marty said.

Christ, Merkle thought. Does the poor son of a bitch know? Is that why he's so blue? Jesus, you'd think he'd kill that spic.

"Anything else I can do?" he asked.

"What?"

"Well, I was just wondering if there was anything else I could do before I left."

"Oh," Marty said, trying to remember what he wanted to tell Merkle. There was something he wanted Merkle to do, and it was important, but he couldn't remember it. Everything was so muddled in his mind. Suddenly it was vital for him to remember, and he gripped the arms of the chair and tried to force his mind back into the present.

Then it came to him. And with it, came a wild exhilaration, a surge of energy almost beyond control.

"Goddam!" he said, jumping up for his chair. "Some bastard is bugging Marsha's place. You find that bug, understand? I want that extortion bit stopped. You get your ass down there and find it."

Merkle quickly assumed what he considered a look of great interest and innocence. "You can trust me, Marty. There won't be any bugs when I get done. You can bet on that."

"Okay, okay," Marty said, already tired of the conversation. "Blow. I've got things to do besides talking to you. This goddam city is blowing up and I stand here talking to an idiot. Blow, man, blow. I've got important business."

Merkle was out of his chair and running, his thin body twisted by the heavy bag, by the time Marty finished talking.

Marty watched him run around the side of the house, then quickly turned around and kicked the canvas chair into the pool.

"Son of a bitch," he cried. "Let's get some goddam action in this goddam dump."

11.

It was three-thirty when Bryce Barker parked the low-slung Ferrari Europa in front of Hollywood High School on Sunset Boulevard and settled down to wait. He lit a cigarette and thought about what he'd say to Alan Avery after all the years. They had been good friends way back before the war in Keene, New Hampshire. That was a long way in time and space.

He heard the bell ring inside the high school and a few

minutes later the doors flew open, disgorging hundreds of teenagers, flooding the lawn and sidewalk, filling the air with their chatter and laughter. Bryce watched them and felt old and useless. Some of the boys whistled when they saw the Ferrari and jostled each other playfully until they were standing before the low-slung car, kidding and laughing, but their eyes full of admiration.

Bryce smiled wistfully. How ironic life was. There he sat, the personification of success, envied and admired by these young men, while he would give everything to be like them, young again, with the whole world ahead, when everything was new and exciting.

Then, almost as quickly as they had come upon the scene, they had disappeared and the sidewalk was empty and quiet again. Bryce lit another cigarette and longed for a drink. He could use one right now. A double Scotch on the rocks. It would relax him, soothe his jangled nerves.

He thought about Diane and felt the passion stir again inside of him. Something important had happened last night. He knew now that his impotence had been due to a mental block. The fear of being impotent had made him impotent. There was no fear now. Only desire. And more desire. He wanted Diane. Wanted her now. But that would have to wait until tonight. Man, he felt as virile as a stallion at a breeding farm.

He looked up and saw Alan Avery coming down the school steps. He recognized him immediately. He looked a lot younger than his picture, almost as young as Bryce remembered him. He was walking next to a heavy-set man, and Bryce noticed how slim Alan was compared to the man. Still the tall, thin kid, he thought. The man was holding Alan's arm and talking, his face red with excitement, his other gesticulating wildly.

Bryce opened the door of the Ferrari and stood on the sidewalk, waiting until Alan and the heavy-set man descended the stone steps and had reached the sidewalk before going up to them.

"Hello, Alan," he said, smiling, his right hand reaching out and taking Alan's hand in a firm grip. "It's been a long time."

"Bryce Barker," Alan said, his face lighting up in that boyish way, his hazel eyes surprised, yet mildly curious. "Well, how are you?"

Barker laughed and pumped Alan's hand fondly. "Fine. You're looking good, kid. Real good."

"Thanks," Alan said, moved by the sudden meeting. "You're looking good yourself. Very prosperous." He brought his other hand over the joined handshake and patted Bryce's hand gently. "It's nice seeing you again."

They stood there, smiling at each other without speaking, until Ralph Henning coughed noisily.

"Oh," Alan said, embarrassed. "This is Ralph Henning. Ralph, meet an old friend of mine, Bryce Barker. We haven't seen each other in about seventeen years."

"Glad to meetcha," Henning said. "Hey, ain'tcha the guy that's defending Ricca?"

The smile left Barker's face and he gave Alan a quick pleading look. "Yes," he said.

"Well," Henning said, "that's a hell of a coincidence."

Barker ignored Henning and spoke to Alan. "Listen, kid, could we get together for a drink or something? I'd like to talk to you. It's important."

"Why, sure," Alan said, and turned to Henning. "Will you excuse me, Ralph? Bryce can take me home."

"Okay with me," Henning said. "Take care of yourself," and he gave Alan a friendly tap on the arm and hurried away, nodding curtly to Barker as he left.

"Well," Alan said, suddenly at a loss for words. "Is that your car out there?"

"I'm afraid so."

"What do you mean afraid so? It's beautiful," he said approaching the car.

"It seems kind of foolish right now."

"I've never ridden in a car like this before," Alan said, ignoring Barker's remark as he peered inside the car.

"Well, by God, you're going to now," Barker laughed, a trifle too loud. "Get in. We're off to someplace. How about the Brown Derby on Vine?"

"My favorite place," Alan laughed. "Go there every day."

Barker pressed the starter and the powerful motor burst into life with a roar, a rich, lush roar that quickly changed into a soft, smooth purr that insinuated countless horses under the hood.

They rode in silence, Barker carefully guiding the big car through the heavy afternoon traffic, his handsome features creased in a frown; and Alan sitting next to him, wondering what Barker will say, hoping it wouldn't be what he suspected. He thought of Edie, too, and made a mental note to call her as soon as they arrived at the Brown Derby.

Barker took him to the Record Room in the Brown Derby, a small cozy room with red leather upholstered booths and white jacketed waiters. The walls were completely covered with pastel portraits of recording artists who had sold over a million discs. There were a lot of them, and they all smiled down benignly from their coveted perch.

Bryce and Alan sat down. While Alan excused himself to telephone Edie, Barker ordered two very dry Martinis. He lit a cigarette and nodded to a television producer and director who had just come into the room.

Then Alan was back and Bryce was looking at him, smiling.

"I hope your wife wasn't too put out with me," he said.

"No, everything's fine. She's expecting, you know. Should be any day now. I don't like leaving her alone any more than I have to."

"What's her name?"

"Edie. You'll have to meet her."

"Is she from Keene?"

"No. I met her right here during the war."

"Any children?"

"No. Just the one on the way."

"What does Edie think of this situation?"

"You mean the baby?"

"No. I mean being a witness."

"Oh. Well, she's a little worried naturally, but she's taking it very well."

"How about you, Alan? Are you taking it well?"

"Yes. I think so."

"Your friend was right, you know. I'm Ricca's attorney."

"Yes, I know. I saw your name in the paper."

"What do you think about my being Ricca's attorney?"

"I don't know. I haven't given it much thought."

"You don't like it, do you?"

"I guess I don't."

"You think I'm pretty low?"

"Well, I think you could have done much better. You were brilliant student. We all had high hopes for you."

"Really?"

"Yes, we did."

"Even when I had a weakling for a father and an alcoholic for a mother, you all had high hopes?"

"Yes."

"How interesting. And even after my old man became a national freak. You still had hopes?"

"I'm sorry," Alan said, sensing the slowly building hysteria under the sharp words. "I didn't mean to bring that up."

"Don't apologize. I brought it up." He leaned forward and emptied the Martini glass. There was another one waiting right next to it and he emptied it also. The waiter was there immediately with a fresh drink. He carried the empty glasses away. He was well trained.

"I, too, had hopes at one time. High hopes. And they all centered around that full scholarship to Yale. Man, I was sitting on top of the world. Nothing could touch me." And he emptied another glass.

"'I know," Alan said. "Remember my visiting you one weekend?"

"Yes, yes," Bryce said, anxious to get on with his thoughts. "And then that stupid old fool had to make an international ass of himself. Imagine, climbing up that church steeple and staying there for over forty-eight hours. The old fool lost his nerve, and the longer he stayed up there, the more impossible it became for him to come down."

"It was very tragic."

"Tragic! You don't know the half of it." And he emptied another glass. "They called me from Yale and forced me up that tower. They wanted me to talk him out of jumping. Well, I went up there and I talked to him, all right. I told him to jump. I screamed at him. I called him every vile name I could think of. I hated him and I wanted him to die. He had disgraced me. Ruined my future. I knew I could never go back to Yale. Not after that."

Alan looked at Barker and saw the tears running down his cheeks. Barker took out his handkerchief and wiped his eyes, then blew his nose. He looked at Alan and tried to smile, but all that happened was a quivering along the jaw-line and he bit down hard on his lip trying to stop it.

"I'm making an ass of myself," he said, looking around the room to see if anyone was watching him. "Alan, I've seen that fall a thousand times. It has become my nightmare. I've gone to an analyst for years, but it's no good. I still see it in every minute detail. Even to how I felt about it. I remember the hatred that swept through me as I looked at him. His face was dirty and his beard was long. There was spittle at the corners of his mouth as he looked at me with those weak, defeated eyes of his, and I wanted to kill him. Then he jumped, and I watched him falling, turning over and over, not making a sound, never even yelling once, and something inside of me snapped. And I cried. Yes, I cried for that stupid old fool who never did one decent thing for me or my mother."

He stopped and dried his eyes again and emptied another Martini glass. He could feel the powerful drinks going to work inside of him, but he didn't care. He wanted to drink himself unconscious.

"Well, as you know, I left Keene a couple of weeks later. I never went back. I came to Los Angeles and went to night school. That's how I got my law degree, working days and going to school at night. But enough about me. Now let's talk about you and your problem."

"I don't have any problem," Alan said.

"Oh, yes, you do," Bryce said, looking up at Alan. "You've got to change your story to the police."

"I can't do that, Bryce."

"But you've got to. Don't you know what you've got yourself into?"

"No. Not really."

"Alan, take my word for it. Your life depends on it. You've got to change your story. Tell the police you were mistaken. You don't remember a thing. Refuse to testify in court. Divorce yourself completely from every aspect of this case."

"Are you threatening me?"

"I'm not threatening you. I'm merely telling you the facts. You figure the rest out for yourself."

Alan sat very still for a moment, toying with his glass, then he turned and looked Bryce squarely in the eyes.

"I'm going to have to take that chance," he said, slowly standing up.

"Sit down, please, Alan. Hear me out."

Alan hesitated for a moment then sat down.

"Alan, you've got to understand what I'm saying. I'm not trying to save Ricca. For all I care he can rot in jail. I'm trying to save you. I know these people and I know that unless you change your story, they're going to kill you."

"I'll get police protection ..."

"Don't be ridiculous. The police can't do a damn thing for you. They'll kill you and when they do, they'll all have perfect alibis. Believe me, Alan. I know what I'm saying."

"I believe you."

"Well, then, how about it?"

"I can't do it."

"Why not?"

"For a lot of reasons. But for now, let's just say that I can't do it because I don't live in that kind of a world."

"Oh, come on. Let's not be stuffy about it."

Alan took a sip of the Martini. He needed something to calm him down. "I won't have gangsters dictate my actions," he said, his voice low and steady. "And that means you, too, Bryce."

"Okay," Barker said, beginning to slur his words. His face was flushed and his eyes were getting that alcoholic haze, as he turned to face Alan. "So I'm a gangster. In your mind, I'm as bad as any of them. All right. Granted. But please listen to me. I'm here as your friend. I want to help you. I am doing my damnedest to save your life. This may sound melodramatic to you, but believe me, it's the truth. You've got to change your story. Alan, be reasonable. What's more important, being dead or compromising just a little?"

Alan stood up. "I think I better be going. I promised Edie I'd be home by five."

"Don't go, Alan. Listen to me ..."

"No. I'm not going to listen anymore."

Barker shook his head in disgust and stood up. "I'll drive you home," he said.

"Don't bother. I'll take a cab."

"Look," Barker said, then shrugged his shoulders and sat down, looking up at Alan. "I've done all I can. It's up to you now. Here's my card. Call me if you change your mind."

"Good night," Alan said, taking the card.

12.

At seven o'clock that evening, Merkle was sitting in the basement of Marsha Brown's call house. It had been a tough day. His visit at Kahn's place had him worried. He would have to be especially careful in the future when dealing with extortion victims. If Kahn ever got wise to him, he was as good as dead.

His first job that evening had been to remove all evidence of a tap on Marsha's line. It would mean more work for him now, but it was going to be a lot safer. He would have to tap directly into the phone line, and it meant that he had to be there to listen to the calls instead of having them recorded on tape in his shop. But that wouldn't be too difficult, since all the important calls came between seven and eight every evening. That was when gentlemen arranged for their evening's entertainment with Marsha's high-class call girls.

The arrangement usually called for a meeting at a

swanky hotel in the Hollywood area. The girl handled all the details, rented the room, provided the liquor and food, and the flesh. All the gentleman needed was the money.

Whenever possible Merkle would rent an adjoining room. Sometimes when the contact was important enough and he couldn't get a room, Merkle would find other means of getting the evidence on tape, and these often led to ingenious innovations.

Now he listened as the telephone rang and Marsha's husky voice came alive in his ear.

"Hollywood 8-4993," she said.

"Marsha. Bobbie here. Can you recommend a good book for tonight?"

"How about something with a redhead heroine. Very sexy."

"Sounds delightful. Where can I get it?"

"Bela-Woods."

"How many pages?"

"Four hundred and thirty-four."

"Great. What else is new?"

"Not much. I read ten books last week."

"Gads! You're so ambitious."

"Gotta keep up, you know."

"Righto. Well, dig you later."

The line went dead and Merkle quickly translated the information: Bela-Woods Hotel, Room 434 at ten o'clock. The redhead would be Niki, a twenty-two-year-old pro with a lot of class. The Bela-Woods was a plush hostelry and Room 434, as Merkle remembered from previous occasions, was a three-room suite, and with a balcony, yet. Bobbie had to be plenty loaded. Merkle smiled. He had his pigeon for tonight. He started to disconnect the tap when the telephone rang again.

"Hollywood 8-4993."

"Marsha?"

"Yeah."

"This is Reggie."

"Don't bother me. I'm busy."

"Hey, wait. How about a good book for tonight?"

"Call the public library."

"Now, Marsha, be a good sport."

"Drop dead."

"You're mad about the check, aren't you?"

"You goddam right."

"I'll make it good. I promise. Friday for sure."

"This is Friday."

"Next Friday."

"Good-by!"

And the line went dead for a few seconds then rang again.

"Yeah."

"Listen, Marsha. My word is good around this town. Friday for sure."

"I don't give a damn about your word. No check, no book."

"I promise. You'll get it Friday. My word of honor."

"Nothing doing. From now on it's cash in advance."

"Okay, Marsha. But how about tonight?"

"No soap."

"Just this once."

"No, no, no."

"Jesus, Marsha, you can't do this to me. I've got myself in the mood. Have a heart."

"Take a cold shower. And don't call me back until that check is in the mail."

Merkle heard the receiver slam down and laughed. Old cash-and-carry Marsha. He stood up and quickly disconnected the tap. He picked up the toolcase and quietly went up the stairs, his small body twisted by the heavy weight.

Every Friday night Marty Kahn watched the fights on television. He watched with the sound turned off, calling out advice to the muted gladiators, snarling when his boy got tagged, cheering wildly when he scored. Between the rounds, Kahn would jump up and start pounding on Little Abner, demonstrating the highlights of the round.

Tonight, when Barker arrived, there were two other men besides Marty and Little Abner in the large walnut-paneled den watching the fights. Round Six was in progress and Barker sat down, knowing that Kahn could not be disturbed in the midst of a fight.

"Wow," Kahn yelled, rising halfway out of his chair. "He about got him that time. Didja see that left? Christ, if only he had the reach. That's what happens to a husky welter. Too short. Look at that other bastard. He's got at least four inches on him. Jesus, didja see that? Right in the old bread basket. Come on, hold up that right. Goddam, man, hold up that right. That skinny bastard will kill you if you don't. Look out! Oh, Christ, right on the button. He's out. Man, he's out for the night."

Kahn jumped out of his chair and took a few fast cuts at Little Abner, who was still sitting down. "Get up, God damn it." And Little Abner scrambled to his feet. "Now, see what I mean," he said, dancing around Little Abner, holding his right up, jabbing with his left, breathing hard and loud through his broken nose.

"When you fight one of them tall bastards, you've got to hold up your right, otherwise he'll clobber you to death. And, man, I know. Every son of a bitch I fought as a welter was at least two inches taller than me. Then I kept putting on weight, and the first goddam thing I knew I was fighting middle. Christ, one night I fought a guy that was over six feet tall. It was like walking into a goddam windmill. Christ, that one was even taller and faster than

Sugar Ray. That was my last fight. I couldn't keep the old weight down. Not that I was fat. Man, I had the biggest chest and shoulders, real powerful, but not enough reach. Wouldn't that frost you, though? I could've killed anyone my height."

And he drove a terrific left and a right into Little Abner's stomach. Little Abner gasped, his big eyes popping out, and stumbled backward, his huge hands grasping his middle. Kahn laughed and saw Barker for the first time.

"For Christ sakes, Doctor, when did you come in?"

"Few minutes ago."

"Why didn't you speak up?"

"Didn't want to spoil the fun," he said, glancing at the two strangers.

"Well, goddam, glad to see you. Here, I want you to meet Jimmy Gracio and Jack Nitta, two old buddies from way back."

Gracio, a tall, handsome middle-aged man in a very sharp single-breasted silk suit stood up and came forward, smiling, holding his hand out to Barker. Bryce smiled and shook the hand, feeling the other man's strength in the firm grip.

"Glad to meet you," Gracio said.

Jack Nitta grunted and waved feebly, without leaving his chair. He was of average height with a thin face and a heavy body. He was pushing well into his sixties.

"I've heard a lot about you," Gracio said, slowly lighting a cigarette. "Marty thinks you're pretty great."

"Thanks," Bryce said, glancing at Marty.

"He's the most," Kahn said, tapping Barker lightly on the arm. "Well, what gives with the creep?"

"The what?"

"The creep. For Christ sakes don't tell me you've forgotten about that stupid teacher?"

"He's hardly a creep," Barker said, resenting the derogatory reference to Alan.

"He's a creep to me," Kahn said. "What goes?"

"I need a little more time."

"For what?"

"You've got to go slow on a fellow like that."

"Can it! He a cousin of yours or something?"

"No," Bryce said, a little too quickly. "It's just that you can't go around knocking off teachers."

"Why not?"

"It would arouse public sentiment," Bryce said, knowing that the remark sounded foolish.

"Screw public sentiment. It ain't ever done nothing for me." Gracio watched the two men, a thin smile playing at the corners of his strong mouth.

"Marty, you've got to be reasonable about this," Barker said. Let's wait for a while. There's plenty of time."

"How about some loot? Maybe that's the answer."

"No. That's not the answer."

"Hey," Nitta said. "Maybe he'd listen to a poke in the head."

Barker glanced at Nitta, then turned around and walked over to the bar and fixed himself a double Scotch on the rocks. His head throbbed and he had a terrible taste in his mouth. Those goddam Martinis, he thought, as he tipped the glass back and quickly gulped it down, the warm liquid burning his throat, bringing tears to his eyes. He stood there, his back to Marty, the room suddenly quiet, and fixed himself another drink.

"You can't solve everything with a poke in the head," he said, turning around to face Jack Nitta.

"Yeah," Nitta snarled. "That's what you think."

"Ricca just killed a witness. Now there's a witness to the killing of the first witness. Where does it stop? You kill everybody?"

"No," Marty said, "not when you've got brains. Now,

I'm gonna show you guys something. Bring him in, Little Abner."

Nitta grunted and glared at Barker. Barker stared back at him, not afraid of the menacing eyes, just bone-tired. He wished he could lie down. He lifted the drink and let the liquid flow down his throat. It felt good this time. Real good. He went back to the bar and mixed himself another drink. When he came back to his chair, Gracio and Nitta were talking in low voices. There was a thin smile playing at the corners of Gracio's mouth as he talked to Nitta, and Bryce knew from the expression on Nitta's face that Gracio was laying the law down.

"God damn it," Kahn said, staring angrily at the open doorway. "What's that son of a bitch doing?"

"What's the big deal?" Gracio asked.

"Never mind," Kahn laughed. "You'll see. By Christ, you'll see who's got the brains in this outfit."

Just then Little Abner came into the room, his huge hand clasped around the neck of a dark, curly-haired man. The man's face was badly bruised and smeared with dried blood. His nose was broken and one of his eyes was swollen completely shut. The other eye surveyed the room fearfully. He held his chest and walked delicately on the balls of his feet as Little Abner pulled him into the room until he stood facing Marty.

"This is Mike Scipio," Marty declared loudly to the room. "A no-good bookie with sticky fingers. How do you feel now, Mike?"

"Not so good," Scipio mumbled through swollen lips. "I'm in bad shape. I need a doctor. I think I've got a couple of busted ribs. I can feel them scratching my lungs."

"That's real tough," Kahn said, assuming a sympathetic expression. "But don't worry; the cops will take good care of you. Now listen carefully while I go over this caper again. You're gonna go down to headquarters and tell the fuzz how Ricca beat you up last night. You and Ricca had a little fight over some broad, see. You got wise and Ricca smacked you around a bit. Tell the fuzz you don't want to prefer charges since you're the guy that started it. Understand?" Kahn clapped his hands proudly and laughed, looking over at Barker.

"How's that for a gimmick, Doctor?"

"Not bad," Barker said, realizing that this could be the answer, the gimmick that took the pressure off Alan Avery.

"Hey, listen to him," Kahn cried. "Not bad! Christ! It's perfect. What do you say, Jimmy?"

"Could be the answer," Gracio said. "If the cops don't check too closely."

"Never mind the checking. They can check all they damn please. This character looks enough like Danchik to be his twin brother. And—this is the real kicker—he's got the same blood type. I checked with a stooge in the crime lab this afternoon. Now, what do you say?"

"Now you're talking," Gracio said.

Nitta grunted approvingly.

Barker was surprised. This was not the action of a crazy man. Kahn was thinking again as he had in the old days when he had carved an empire out of a jungle.

Kahn's eyes sparkled with excitement as he gripped Scipio by the shirt front. "You better do it right if you want to stay alive in this town."

"Just a minute," Barker said. "I'd like to make a couple of suggestions."

"Sure, Doctor, go ahead." Kahn was always magnanimous in his glory.

Barker stood up and walked over to Marty, feeling the tension of the last twenty-four hours suddenly lift.

"First, I think he should turn in at Georgia Street Receiving Hospital. Then once he's admitted, he can ask for the police. You know, he wants to make a clean breast of it. He should be angry, anxious for revenge, ready to prefer charges. It will look better this way. I'll have Ricca and Doto out on bail within two hours. Now, the other thing is when the arraignment comes up in about a week. He should appear determined to give Joe the business right up to the time he's standing before the judge. Then he can have a change of heart. In the name of justice, he must confess that he was really at fault. He's the one who started the whole thing. Now he wishes to retract his statement, Ricca and Doto are good guys. He's sorry for all the trouble he's caused. See what I mean?"

"I buy it," Kahn said, smiling happily. "But you don't ever forget whose idea this was."

"How about the throat," Nitta said. "The papers said Joe slit the guy's throat."

"For Christ sakes," Kahn said. "I want a witness, not a stiff."

"We'll just cut it a little bit," Nitta said. "To make it look good. Can't take any chances, you know."

"Sure," Gracio said. "Jack is real slick with a blade."

Scipio tried to wrench himself out of Little Abner's grasp. He was breathing hard and fast, his good eye shifting wildly from Kahn to Nitta to Gracio and back again.

"How about the bleeding? This gotta look like it happened last night," Kahn said.

"Got some collodion?" Gracio asked.

"That's it," Kahn said, slowly and almost affectionately pushing his fist across Scipio's chin. "Don't worry, Mike. It won't hurt. Not much!" He laughed into Scipio's panic-stricken face.

"You guys are kidding," Scipio mumbled.

"Sure," Marty said.

"Yeah," Nitta said, standing up, the switch-blade knife suddenly in his hand, a fierce smile on his thin face as he approached Scipio.

"Don't," Scipio screamed, struggling wildly against Little Abner's iron grip.

"Hold his head back," Nitta said. "And keep it steady."

"Wait," Kahn said. "I don't want any blood on the carpet. Get some newspapers, Little Abner."

Nitta stuck the knife against Scipio's chest while Little Abner ran out of the room to get the newspapers.

Barker had watched the proceeding, horrified, unable to believe that they were actually going to carry it out, the rumbling in his stomach getting louder with every word that brought the action closer.

"I have to go," he said.

"Take it easy," Nitta said. "Stay for the fun."

"I can't be a witness to this," Barker said. "My job is to defend Ricca, and I can't very well do that if I get implicated in this business."

"Implicated!" Gracio sneered. "That's a goddam laugh."

"Stick around, Doctor," Marty said, his eyes bright, his pudgy face flushed.

"I'm going," Barker said, not moving, glaring at Marty.

"I said stick around."

"Be reasonable, Marty," Barker said, starting to edge toward the door. "What good can I be to you here?"

"Don't argue with me. I said stick around and that's what I mean. So park your ass over there and sit."

"Go to hell," Barker shouted, suddenly and furiously trembling with rage. "I'm not your goddam slave. Murder and mayhem is your dirty business. Not mine! I'm leaving and don't try to stop me." Perspiration had broken out all over his body and he had difficulty focusing on the people in the room. But his shoulders were erect and his head high as he strode out of the room.

"Come back here," Kahn shouted, quickly moving toward the now empty doorway. "You son of a bitch. You creepy, deaf bastard. Come back here!" And he rushed out of the room, his big eyes wild with frustration.

But once out of the den, away from the others, he stopped as he heard the front door slam shut behind Barker. He still had time to catch Barker if he hurried, but he waited, waited until he heard the full-throated roar of the Ferrari, and the loud, hurried meshing of the gears, before rushing out of the house. He felt confused again, and he fought the depression trying to engulf him. Barker had him worried and he resented it, resented the thought that he, Marty Kahn, needed anyone. That anyone was important to him.

"You lousy bastard," he shouted at the disappearing taillights, then still cursing, he turned around and ran into the house. When Marty re-entered the den, the macabre scene was already set. The newspapers were thickly spread out under Mike Scipio, and Little Abner had him stretched out across his knee in a judo hold. By applying pressure against the stomach and chest, Little Abner was able to bend Scipio's back around his knee almost to the breaking point. Gracio held a handful of dark wavy hair in a tight fist, bringing the head back, leaving the throat fully exposed.

Nitta held the knife a few inches away from Scipio's throat and laughed. Bubbles were forming at the corners of Scipio's mouth, and his one good eye showed only white. Then, just as the knife touched his throat, he fainted. His sphincter muscles lost control, and there was a loud dripping sound on the newspapers. Nitta looked up at Kahn and winked.

"Get going," Gracio said. "I'm not gonna stand here all night."

"Okay, okay," Nitta said, and brought the blade against the tight brown skin and pressed down, swiftly moving the knife completely across the full throat before the red blood spurted out.

"How's that?" Nita said, examining his handiwork.

Gracio grinned at Kahn and shook his head admiringly. "That old bastard can really handle a blade."

"Yeah," Kahn said, "very pretty. Now get the collodion on and let's get this show on the road."

Nitta picked up the bottle which was lying at his feet and quickly coated the wound with the gummy liquid, sealing off the bleeding.

"Now you've got yourself a real witness," Nitta said, wiping the knife blade on Scipio's trousers.

"Yeah, yeah," Kahn said, turning to Little Abner, feeling himself slipping deeper into the depression.

"Get the bastard into the shower and clean him up good, then drive him out to George Street."

"Well," Gracio said, moving across to the bar. "How about a drink?"

"Not for me," Kahn said. "I've got some business to take care of. You guys make yourselves comfortable until Joe shows up."

Gracio turned and studied Kahn for a moment, the smile back on his lips. "I thought we could have a little talk."

"We'll talk," Kahn said. "Later." And hurried out of the room. He had to get by himself and fight the depression. Then he'd have to think about Barker and figure out something. Everybody was getting out of line, and Marty Kahn was losing his hold. Christ, what a lousy goddam setup. He'd have to start all over again. Rebuild the whole organization from the ground up. He'd show them, by Christ. He'd show every goddam bastard that Marty Kahn was big. The biggest son of a bitch that ever lived.

13.

Wearing a black pin-stripe double-breasted suit, a black homburg, patent-leather shoes, white gloves, and carrying an ebony walking stick, Merkle casually strolled across the plush lobby of the Bela-Woods and stepped into the waiting elevator. It was nine forty-five when he got out on the fourth floor. Having been unable to acquire an adjoining room, Merkle had dressed to fit the demands of the situation. There was a tiny hearing-aid receiver in his right ear and a thin wire hung from it, disappearing under a stiffly starched collar. From there the wire was pulled over his shoulder and down his chest, then through a small hole in the front of his shirt and finally plugged into a miniature wire recorder carried in the inside pocket of his suit jacket. Another thin wire ran down the inside of his coat sleeve and into the head of the walking stick. The ebony stick itself was one of Merkle's most ingenious inventions. It housed a sensitive microphone and powerful amplifier. By merely holding the stick against a wall, Merkle was able not only to hear the slightest sound inside the room, but also to record it.

Merkle stood before the closed door of the elevator and adjusted his tie while he quickly surveyed the empty hallway. Room 434 was three doors down, and he moved to the opposite side of the elevator and leaned against the wall. He took out a coin and dropped it on the thick carpet. Now he had a reason for standing there. If anyone came up, he could busy himself looking for the coin.

Ten minutes later he heard the elevator stop and the doors open. Slowly, he leaned forward in search of the coin. He waited until the elevator doors had closed before daring a furtive look. The man was short and portly with a shock of white hair that was long and shaggy. He must have been close to sixty, a pink-skinned, blue-eyed sixty. There was a smile on his face as he glanced at Merkle. Then, whistling softly between clenched teeth, he hurried up the hall to Room 434.

Merkle had no trouble recognizing him. It was Robert Redford, one of the greatest comedians ever to make the grade. This guy had been great for forty years, and he was still riding the crest of success. Merkle smiled. It was going to be a profitable evening.

At that exact moment, Ernie Tucker was standing before the locked door to Merkle's shop. Tucker's curiosity had been aroused by the muffled sound behind the partition he had heard that morning. He had thought about it all day. And the more he thought about it, the more convinced he had become about its source. Especially when he considered Merkle's reputation.

Now, as he stood before the dirty plate-glass window of Merkle's shop, he knew that whatever he found in there would be important. Maybe even important enough to risk an illegal-entry charge.

He waited for the traffic to thin out before going to work on the lock. It was a regular spring lock, the kind that was simple enough to pick if you knew how. And after nineteen years on the force, Ernie Tucker knew how.

It was a cool, clear night, the kind you get in Los Angeles after a hot fall day. The smog had lifted and there was a clean smell to the brisk air. Tucker walked up to the door and stopped. There was a car coming and he waited for it to pass before inserting the pick. Thirty seconds later the door swung open and Tucker hurried inside.

He closed the door and carefully made his way through the darkness to the heavy door of the partition and the huge combination lock. He had spent the better part of the afternoon fashioning a pick for the lock, a small iron rod with a long, extremely thin, curved piece of metal at the end that was shaped almost like a bent spoon. Now he slipped the curved metal down the shackle of the lock, feeling it depress the little bolts that pressed into the grooves of the bow. He worked slowly, careful not to bend the soft metal of the pick. Suddenly there was a sharp click and the shackle jumped out of the lock.

Tucker grinned. It had worked. He slipped the lock off the clamp and opened the door. Now he would know, and he hoped he had been right. What he needed was evidence against Merkle. Good, strong evidence. Strong enough to force Merkle into doing what he wanted.

There were no windows in the partitioned room and Tucker closed the door and took out his flashlight to look for the light switch. He quickly found it next to the door and flipped it on.

It was a small room, not any larger than the average bathroom. But Tucker was not interested in its size. What he saw were three tape recorders and dozens of reels of tape stacked on top of each other on the bench near the now silent machines. Quickly, he gathered up the reels and began stuffing them into all his pockets until his clothes bulged in all directions. Now all he needed was a machine to play the tapes. He took one on his way out.

Lieutenant Sam Johnson was not a gullible man. In fact, just the opposite was true. Sam Johnson was skeptical and untrusting, unless the facts, the iron-bound facts, were presented for his minute inspection and examination.

Scipio's story went off like a lead balloon. Johnson grunted, frowned, scowled, bit his lip, narrowed his colorless eyes, clenched his fist, blew his nose, rubbed his brow, scratched his butt, stood up, sat down, paced the floor, but never once shouted at Scipio, or even indicated his disbelief.

Scipio, Johnson felt, had had a rough enough time for a while, and besides, nothing could be gained by it. True or false, Scipio was the best thing he had for the time being. Johnson knew the D.A. well enough to know that he would not prosecute a murder case without a corpse. At least, this way they had an assault case with intent to kill. No kidnaping charge would be made since Scipio insisted that Ricca took him home in the trunk because he was unconscious and bleeding. The assault charge was enough to give Johnson a little more time to look for Danchik.

Nevertheless, Johnson wanted verification of his doubts. He had been a cop long enough to know that a hunch is one thing, good enough sometimes, but never good enough when you have access to facts. Facts that could verify your hunch or discredit it. Now, he wanted the facts.

It was two o'clock when he called Alan Avery and asked him to come down to Georgia Street Receiving Hospital. A squad car was sent to pick him up and a very tired, almost gray, Alan Avery walked into the reception room of the hospital half an hour later. Johnson nodded his head in greeting and took him to one side to explain the situation.

"All I want you to do is look at this character. Don't say anything. Just look at him and see if he's the same guy Ricca beat up. That's all I want. Don't say anything in that room."

"All right," Alan said, and followed Johnson into the room.

There were two uniformed policemen in the room, standing by the bed. One of them was leaning forward, lighting Scipio's cigarette. Scipio's face was pretty much bandaged up. His nose had been straightened and the nostrils were stuffed with cotton. A wide piece of tape ran across the bridge of the nose and stopped under the eyes. His forehead was bandaged, and his throat was covered by a thick roll of gauze. His blood-smeared face had been cleaned and the cuts and bruises treated. His one good eye was open and staring at Alan, almost defiantly. No one had told him, but he knew who Alan was, and how important the next few minutes would be. Scipio had no doubts as to what would happen to him if his story didn't take.

"Who's the tourist?" Scipio asked, nodding his head sideways at Alan.

Hearing his voice surprised Alan. This was not the voice he had heard pleading for mercy in the parking lot. It was gruff and gravel-toned, with a thick Italian accent. There were other things that Alan remembered, too; things like the knife cutting open the throat and the blood gushing out. The then lifeless body being pulled off the roof of the car and dropping to the hard asphalt with a bone-crushing sound. This was not the man and Alan was convinced of it, just as convinced as he had been the night before that the man had been murdered before his very eyes.

They came out of the room and walked down the hall without speaking. Johnson had watched Alan's reactions in the room and he had also seen the fear in Scipio's eye.

"Well," he said, "is that the man?"

"No," Alan said. "I'm sure he's not."

"Why not?"

"The man in the parking lot was killed."

"How can you be so sure of that?"

"I'm positive."

"Why? Have you ever seen a man killed before?"

"No. Except in an automobile accident. But I'm positive just the same. I saw that knife cut his throat. Nobody could live with a cut like that. His head just hung all the way back, as if it was held by only a few hairs. Lieutenant, believe me, that man was dead."

"Why should I believe you instead of Scipio? He claims to have been the man. Can you think of any reason why he would want to do that if he wasn't the man?"

"I don't know," Alan said. "It may be a trick."

"I think you're wrong," Johnson said. "You're building the whole thing up in your mind."

"What are you getting at?" Alan asked, frowning at Johnson. "You asked me to come down and see if I could identify this man. I say he's not the same man. His voice is different, too. I heard the other man pleading for his life. He had a high-pitched voice."

"Maybe cutting his throat has changed his voice. Could be, huh?"

"Maybe," Alan said. "But it wouldn't account for the Italian accent."

"Thank you, Mr. Avery," Johnson said. "I'll let you know if I need you anymore."

"Well," Alan said. "What are you going to do?"

"Do? Nothing."

"Are you going to let Ricca out of jail?"

"He's already out. His lawyer sprung him an hour ago."

"I see," Alan said, and he could feel the hair rising on the back of his neck. "Then you believe this man's story?"

"Why not?" Johnson said. "He's a convincing enough witness."

"Good night," Alan said, suddenly in a hurry to get away from this stupid man.

"Yeah," Johnson said, "see you later."

The reporters were in the reception room and when they saw Alan come down the hallway, they stood up and waited for him.

"Mr. Avery," called one of the reporters Alan had seen the night before. "How about giving us a couple of answers?"

"I'm in a hurry," Alan said, thinking of Edie alone at home, suddenly sick of the whole thing, yet angry that Johnson had dismissed it so easily.

"It won't take a second," the reporter said. "Is Scipio the man you saw in the parking lot last night?"

Alan looked at all the reporters before answering.

"No," he said. "That's not the man. The man in the parking lot was murdered. He's dead."

There was a quick exchange of looks among the reporters. "Well, Mr. Avery," one of the reporters asked. "What do you plan on doing now?"

"I plan to go home," Alan said, pushing his way through the crowding reporters. "I've told the police what I know. The rest is up to them. Good night."

After getting Ricca and Doto out on bail, Bryce Barker went to his apartment, took off the hearing aid, changed into pajamas, and brought a fifth of Scotch to bed with him. He felt like getting drunk. Real stinking drunk. The talk with Alan that afternoon had brought back all the old memories and the bottle was the only thing that could push them back again where they belonged. He tilted the bottle back and the warm liquid rushed down his open throat, his Adam's apple bobbing up and down with each gulp, some of it running down the corners of his open mouth. There were tears in his eyes when he brought the bottle down, and for a few seconds he had difficulty breathing. But soon it felt good. Warm and relaxing.

He thought of his mother and wondered what had happened to her, He had never written to her, had not even seen her once in seventeen years. She used to take a bottle to bed with her, too, he remembered. Maybe she had had something to forget. Maybe she was trying to forget she had married his father. Well, whatever it was, she had consumed her share of liquor. He couldn't remember a day since the age of twelve when she had been completely sober.

Then he reflected on his own life, and how everything had misfired. His life, with all the money and all the luxuries money could buy, was nothing. And had been nothing for as many years as he could remember.

All those years in school had been torture. The kids had laughed at him, poked fun at the big ugly wooden box he carried around as a hearing aid. He had never played games, had always sat on the sidelines, watching, sick with envy.

Alan had been his only friend, the only person who had taken the time to understand him. And yet Alan had never been sympathetic. He had always treated Bryce as an equal, never considering his hearing impairment as a handicap. They had played together. Games that did not require sharp hearing. They had played cards and checkers, and then later they had played chess. They had spent many wonderful evenings playing chess, eating cheese and crackers and drinking that wonderful lemonade Mrs. Avery used to make. Those had been the best days of his life. The two years at Yale had also been good. But only because they led to something better. They were the means to an end, and Bryce had buried himself in his school work, staying away from all social activities. It could all wait until later. Until he was famous. Then he'd have time for playing. But until then, everything was going to be work, and more work.

He tilted the bottle up again and took a deep gulp. Oh, it felt good. It was escape. How well Barker knew that. With his knowledge of psychology, there was always the deeper meaning there to irritate him, but lately he hadn't cared. Escape was what he wanted and as long as liquor could give it to him, he would take it. When it stopped providing an escape, then he'd look for something else.

He thought about this often now, and in the back of his mind, he knew what the something else was going to be, but he never allowed it to come to his conscious mind. For now the liquor was doing a satisfactory job as long as he took enough of it. That was the trouble with all escapes. It was only temporary. Sooner or later, you had to come back to the reality of the moment. And you came back from the glorious escape, weak and sick, totally unprepared for the unwanted reality.

As Barker drank, he had noticed the light flashing on a table by his bed and he had felt the vibration of the bed, but he had ignored it. This was the system he had had installed to tell him when the phone was ringing. He didn't feel like getting up or talking to anyone. He had some decisions to make, decisions that would change his life. He reached back and took a pad and pencil from the top of the headboard. He had to find out how much he was worth at this very minute in cold cash. There was about eighty-two thousand dollars in the bank. He had about a dozen government bonds worth about eight thousand, and about fifteen thousand in various stocks.

He could forget the ten thousand he had spent decorating and furnishing the apartment. Nobody paid anything for second-hand furniture. To hell with it. He'd give it to the Salvation Army. They'd have a ball with this fugitive setting from a science-fiction movie.

There was the Ferrari. Had cost him close to twenty thousand. It was two years old now. Maybe worth about five or six thousand. Then there was the cabin cruiser. Had cost him close to sixty thousand four years ago. Maybe he could get twenty.

How much did it all add up to? One hundred and thirty thousand dollars. A pretty small nest egg for a guy who had earned over a million taxable income in the last ten years, plus half a million that never saw a tax form.

He threw the paper and pencil on the floor and tilted the bottle. Could he really quit? Would Kahn allow it? Should he talk to Kahn about it, or should he just take off. Maybe he could phone Kahn and tell him just before taking off. He could say, "Hey, Marty, old friend, I'm quitting." No, he shouldn't say old friend. Maybe, old boy. No, not that either. How about: "Hey, Marty, you old bastard, I'm quitting, see. And I don't want no lip. Understand?"

That sounded better. He took another drink. The way he felt now, anything was possible. To hell with it. He wasn't going to worry about Marty Kahn. If he wanted to quit, he'd quit. That's all there was to it.

He had done their dirty work for ten years. That was long enough for any man. Let them make somebody else rich for a while. Give some other fresh, ambitious law-school grad a chance at fame and fortune.

What good was the goddam money anyway? What had it done for him? He hadn't been anywhere except Las Vegas and San Francisco, and that had usually been on business. He had never gone to Europe. By God, that's what he would do now. Go to Europe. Rent a chalet in the Swiss Alps and stay there for a couple of years. Read and rest. Just take it easy. Learn to ski even. Hell, he wasn't too old. Let the bastards kill themselves off here in Los Angeles. Because that was what was going to happen, and damn soon, too. Marty Kahn was finished. He had outgrown himself. He was bigger than his brain or ability. He was like the ancient dinosaur, too big to survive. Barker raised the nearly empty bottle and killed it.

14.

Edie had plenty to think about as she lay awake next to Alan. He was sleeping now, a deep, tired sleep that looked almost like death. She knew how tired he was and she knew in her heart that he was sick. Something was seriously wrong and the very fact that he had kept it away from her frightened her more than anything he could possibly have told her. These had been days of fear. Days when there were so many fears she didn't know which fear was stabbing at her. There were the migraine and the baby. That had been bad enough. Now there was that horrible man Ricca, and most frightful of all, Alan was ill.

She moved slightly, careful not to disturb Alan, her large stomach making her movements clumsy and difficult, and for a moment she felt a movement way down in her stomach, almost like someone kicking lightly against her pelvic bone, except that it was from the inside. It frightened her. She couldn't get used to the idea that there was another human being inside of her, a child that would emerge from her body, alive and kicking. A being that had been conceived and nourished within her. Whenever she touched her stomach and felt movement inside, she felt strange. Even the skin didn't feel the same. It was stretched tight and almost insensitive to her touch. At these times she would pray. Pray for strength and guidance. But tonight she had too much to think about. Too many fears to even articulate a prayer.

She wished that Alan had gone along with Lieutenant Johnson. It could have meant the end of this horrifying nightmare. And she raised herself now and looked at his sleeping face, the eyes closed, the mouth slightly open, breathing deeply, and she wanted to put her arms around him and protect him, protect him from what he was doing to himself. She wished she could make him understand how she felt about it, and how frightened she really was. But that was no good, either. Alan was quiet and easygoing, and like most quiet and easygoing people, he took his responsibilities seriously, and once set upon a course, nothing could deter or sway him.

She understood how he felt. She knew he was right believing that you couldn't compromise your principles. You couldn't give in to fear. And, yet, living was the most important thing of all to her. It was better to live, even under gangsters' terms, than to die. She knew that was a cowardly way of looking at it, but she didn't care. Life was too short to quibble about words or principles, much less to die for them.

She was certain, though, that something horrible was going to happen to Alan. And there was nothing she could do about it. All she could do was wait and pray. And suddenly she closed her eyes tightly and started to pray, her lips moving quickly as the words flashed through her fearful mind.

The depression had lifted by the time Ricca and Doto arrived at Kahn's place. They were all in the den now, listening to Marty as he paced nervously up and down the room, his short, stocky legs almost running to keep up with him, stopping at times to pound a clenched fist into an open hand, then starting up again, the words tripping over each other as they escaped from his fat lips.

It had finally happened. Marty Kahn was meeting the showdown. New York wanted to put in the squeeze and Marty Kahn was telling them why they couldn't do it.

"I'm not buying any of that crap. No, sir. Who the hell do you think I am? Some young punk who don't know his ass from his armpit? I'm running this town, and if you bastards want it, you're gonna have to fight for it. I'm not laying down for nobody. And you can tell that to New York for me."

Gracio crossed his leg, pulling his trouser leg up to protect the crease, and smiled, a thin smile that only betrayed the hard eyes.

"I don't want to argue about this," he said. "We're bringing the wire service into California. We're getting cooperation from up north. Now, if it's a fight you want, you'll get it."

"For Christ sakes, Marty," Ricca said. "Listen to Jimmy's proposition."

Kahn whirled and glared at Ricca. "Whose side are you on?"

"I only asked you to listen. Don't get so goddam excited"

"Listen, you bastard, you'd still be in jail if it weren't for me. So let me handle this."

"Look," Gracio said. "You're exaggerating. All we ask is for you to buy the service. Hell, it's gonna be a big help to you. Speed things up."

"Yeah," Kahn said. "I know all about wire services. Don't try to con me."

"Let's give it a try," Ricca said. "I know these boys. They're okay. Hell, this could be a big thing for us. You know the trouble we've been getting running the drops without a service. We lose a lot of business by closing too early before a race. It cuts down on our percentage. Christ, the wire service will pay for itself in the long run."

"What the hell's wrong with you?" Kahn shouted. "Don't you know what they're after? Jesus, are you stupid all of a sudden? I've been in this business long enough to know you can't fight the goddam wire service."

"Okay," Gracio said, standing up. "I've had enough of this quibbling. Now, I'm gonna tell you something. You're a nobody. Understand? A nobody! You've operated in L.A. only because we've let you. Now, we want in. And, believe me, we're gonna get in. We're not gonna stall around any longer."

The words took Kahn by surprise and he stopped in the center of the room, and stared at Gracio, his mouth open, his clenched fists held stiffly at his sides.

"Oh, yeah," he said, his pudgy face red and defiant. "Well, by Christ, I'm the biggest nobody you'll ever know if you start fooling around. I've run this town for ten years. I started with nothing. I had to fight for every goddam thing I've got. This goddam town was a jungle when I started out. Everybody was running a racket, but nobody was bossing anything. I took over one little racket after another, until I had a big racket. And now I've got the whole racket, every piece of it, under wrap. No son of a bitch is gonna take it away from me. Nobody."

"That's all I've got to say," Gracio said, nodding to Nitta, who stood up and strolled over to his side, his shoulders swaying arrogantly. "Sleep over it. I'll call you tomorrow."

"Don't waste my time. You've got your answer."

Gracio didn't answer. He turned around and casually strolled out of the room with Nitta right behind him.

By six o'clock on Saturday morning, Sergeant Ernie Tucker had listened to eight hours of recorded tapes. He knew it would take him at least a week to go through all the reels, but by now he knew it would be worth it.

His luck had been phenomenal. This was much more than he had expected. So far he had heard enough to start a first-class grand jury investigation. All he needed now was the tie-in between Finch and Marsha.

All the tapes had been made on automatic recorders, activated by sound. There was no dead time on the tapes, and at first, it was confusing to Tucker, since one conversation, perhaps taken hours earlier, would run right into a later one. He also had difficulty making out who was speaking, except for voices familiar to him or where names were mentioned.

He listened now to the voice of Marty Kahn:

Kahn: (on the telephone) Listen, General, this is getting ridiculous ... Yeah, that's right. Those are the legit businesses ... the LAPD has no right to question my customers ... Hell, they wait outside my cleaning places and question the customers when they come out ... That's right ... Okay, General....

Kahn: (another telephone call) Johnny, this is Marty ... Yeah ... Fine ... Hey, about that setup I was talking to you about the other day ... Yeah, that's right ... No, just for the movie people ... One crap table, one blackjack table, one roulette wheel ... that's all ... Need some good steerers ... Who? ... Yeah, he should be okay ... Steered for us in Palm Springs ... Get some hungry actor ... Always good at that ... Need some shills, too, for first couple nights ... We don't want anybody to think it's a dead game ... Yeah, don't worry ... Everything is covered.

Kahn: (radio playing in background) my head is killing me. You should have been with me today, Doctor. I was laying off at seven tracks from twenty to thirty G's a track. Then at three o'clock, four or five results came in at the same time and I got a terrific pain in the back of my head ... I've had a headache ever since.

Barker: Did you take some aspirin?

Kahn: About a dozen of 'em. I still got it, though.

Barker: How did you make out?

Kahn: Not bad. I have five grand on a long shot that came in and paid forty-three for two.

Barker: You have no right to a headache. You should be

out celebrating.

(End of tape. Tucker put on a new one.)

Marie: (on telephone) Hello ... Oh, Gloria, I was just gonna call you ... No, Marty is still sleeping ... I know it's late ... what? ... That's right, he went out to Cliff Spar's place ... Yeah, you know, the movie star ... They really have a ball at his place ... That's right ... He's the guy who was that mean gangster in *Red Violence* ... Yeah, me, too. I just love the way he squints his eyes when he's mad ... Oh, yeah ... He's a good friend of Marty ... Sure, I know him ... Comes here often ... Never mind ... Who? ... Bryce Barker ... I haven't forgotten ... He's the most ... A real living doll ... What? You crazy ... Marty would kill me ... (laughs) That's right ... He can't stop me from dreaming ... Oh, but he's real nice ... You know, the way he looks at me sometimes ... I just get goosebumps all over ... Naw, I don't mind the hearing aid ... I had a sweet dream about him again the other night ... (giggles nervously) ... It wasn't like it is with Marty ... You know, just like in a book ... Real cool.

Tired of insignificant chatter, Tucker flipped the speed switch and stopped halfway through the reel.

Ricca: This ain't no ordinary gang war. I remember the time I was sent to Chicago during the war between the Irish and the Wops. I was a machine-gun man in them days. Now, that was a gang war. I found so many of my old buddies on both sides that I couldn't do the job. So I called Lucky and he told me to come back to Brooklyn.

Doto: That's right. I was a shotgun in them days.

Kahn: That's what I need in this outfit. A good shotgun.

Ricca: I know a pretty good boy. He's out in Cleveland right now. This guy carried a little sawed-off shotgun with him all the time.

Kahn: Can we get him?

Ricca: I'll call him first thing in the morning.

Kahn: Talk to Gus. Tell him to buy him a new Caddy, or anything he wants ... Okay?

Ricca: Yeah that oughtta please him.

Kahn: How about the juice? I don't like the way the LAPD is handling our boys.

Ricca: We're gonna have to spread it thicker on top.

Kahn: I don't know what gives ... The gangster squad knocked over my setup in Studio City last night.

Ricca: Hell, those guys are real sorry about that. They're making full restitution.

Kahn: Well, why knock the goddam joint over in the first place?

Ricca: They knocked it over because of the guns in the place.

Kahn: Christ sakes! You can't have a thirty-thousand bankroll without guns.

Tucker turned the machine off and removed the reel. He had to find something about Finch. There had to be a connection somewhere. He started four more reels before hitting paydirt. He turned up the sound and sat down.

Marsha: Hi, Freddie ... You know who. Another one of my clients been hit ... Five G's this time.

Finch: That's no concern of mine.

Marsha: You're supposed to protect me, ain't you?

Finch: Not from that.

Marsha: I'm gonna cut down the staff.

Finch: Why?

Marsha: I don't like the way things are going. I talked to Marty and he's for it.

Finch: I still want my hundred per.

Marsha: Sure, honey ... the operation is gonna be cut in

half.

Finch: Don't be stupid. If you don't run it somebody else will.

Marsha: No they won't. You'll see to that.

Finch: There's no need for you to cut down. You keep things going and I'll get to work on that extortion.

Marsha: You better work fast. Marty's an impatient guy.

Finch: Damn it, Marsha. Don't needle me.

Marsha: Now, honey, don't get mad at little Marsha. I missed you so much this past week. Why haven't you been up to see me?

Finch: I've been busy. I'll be up tonight.

Marsha: Do you still love me?

Finch: Sure.

Marsha: Say it.

Finch: For Christ sakes, Marsha. Grow up.

Marsha: Don't bother coming up tonight if you can't even say you love me.

Finch: Okay, I do.

Marsh: You do what?

Finch: Jesus! I love you. Okay? Is that better?

Marsha: (Giggles) That's better. I'll be waiting for you.

Finch: I might be late.

Marsha: How late?

Finch: I'll be there around midnight.

Marsha: (Heavy breathing) Don't be too late. Be seeing you, lover.

Finch: Bye.

Marsha: (Low and Throaty) Bye-bye, lover.

This was perfect. There was no doubt that the voices on the tape were those of Marsha Brown and Lieutenant Fred Finch of the Vice Squad. This tape was different from the ones taken at Kahn's home. It was made from a telephone tap instead of a room bug, and therefore gave both sides of the conversation. Tucker sat down and smiled at the machine. Wonderful little gadget, he thought.

15.

The Saturday morning newspapers hit the sidewalks like a thunder clap. Alan Avery and Joe Ricca had made the front page again, but even more important was an editorial on the front page of the *Los Angeles Tribune* demanding an immediate grand jury investigation of local criminal activities and influences, and specifically of the recent Ricca fracas.

The eight-column headline was based on Alan's brief statement to the reporters early that morning denying that Scipio was the victim, and was followed by a subhead saying that the real victim had been murdered before his eyes. The story followed:

> Alan Avery, the Hollywood High School teacher who witnessed the beating and knifing of an unidentified man in a Hollywood parking lot Friday morning, denied early today that Jack Scipio was that victim.
>
> Scipio turned himself in at Georgia Street Receiving Hospital last night and stated that he was the man attacked by Joseph Ricca and Abe Doto, both Marty Kahn henchmen, now being held on suspicion of murder and kidnaping in the case.
>
> Scipio, an ex-convict and gambler, was questioned by police in his hospital room, where earlier he had been treated for a sizable number of bruises and slashes about his body.
>
> In his explanation to authorities, Scipio stated

that he was involved in a fist fight which developed over a girl known by him and Ricca. He said he had struck Ricca earlier that evening and Ricca had waited for him in the parking lot to settle the argument. Another fight ensued there, and he said that after the fight, Ricca drove him home. Later on, he said, the bruises and cuts began to hurt and he decided to report to the hospital.

Police expressed skepticism at the story, but changed the murder and kidnaping booking against Ricca and Doto to a charge of suspicion of assault. Both men were later released on writs of habeas corpus which are returnable Monday in Department 42, Superior Court.

Alan Avery was brought to the hospital in a squad car for a look at Scipio and a possible identification. The tall, boyish-looking teacher was positive in his opinion that Scipio was not the man he saw beaten Friday morning.

The editorial in the *Tribune* was something else again. This was what Marty Kahn would be calling "dynamite," the kind of story that put the lid on all underworld activities for a while, and on a few activities it put the lid on for good. This was heat of the worst kind for both cops and robbers. The editorial was titled: "We Need A Cleanup," and it was the kind of angry editorial apt to bring sweeping reforms in its wake.

Tucker read the newspaper at his favorite café, while having his favorite breakfast. He hadn't slept all night, but he felt good. Real good. He glanced down at his foot and saw the all green canvas satchel and smiled. Captain Olin Martin of Intelligence had a surprise coming to him this morning.

Rita brought the plates over and put them down in front of him.

"That's more like it," she said, sternly. "You had me worried yesterday. I thought sure you was sick."

"Well, I'm not sick today," Tucker said, looking hungrily at the half-dozen poached eggs, the three thick slices of fried ham and the stack of pancakes. There also was a side order of toast and a large portion of strawberry preserves. And at his right elbow stood a full silex of steaming coffee.

"Your eyes are kinda bloodshot," she said, peering into his eyes.

"That's because I didn't get any sleep."

"Well, what's so new about that?"

"I mean I didn't get any sleep all day and night."

"Well," Rita said, placing her hands on her hips. "That's kinda stupid. You're no chicken anymore, you know."

"I know," Tucker said, and pressed his fork into the egg, and brought half of it into his mouth. "You don't have to tell me that," he said. "I've known it for years."

"Well, you don't act like it."

"Where's the newspaper?" he asked.

"Coming right up," she said, hurrying back to the counter to pick it up. "There seems to be a lot of screaming about this killing in Hollywood," she said, handing him the paper.

Tucker took in the headline and frowned. His eyes hurried down the column, his quick mind sorting out the facts, analyzing, reading between the lines here and there. Then he skimmed through the editorial.

Well, finally, at long last, there would be some action. Why was it that nothing was ever done without an angry newspaper screaming for blood. And the *Tribune* was really out for blood this time. Well, if they were mad now, just wait until they heard those tapes. Things would really move then.

But how about Alan Avery? From the looks of things, he was in trouble. The worst kind of trouble that Tucker could imagine. One defenseless little teacher standing against a crime organization. One word and there would be a gun aimed at his head, a knife plunged into his heart, a bomb tossed into his home.

What kind of a chance did the law-abiding citizen have against the men who answered to no law?

Tucker thought about Avery, remembered the tall, thin man with the grim, determined expression. He would have to protect him to the best of his ability. Maybe if he passed the word around that Avery was his baby it might do some good.

He resumed eating; when he had finished he folded the paper and placed it on the edge of the table. He moved his foot and touched the canvas satchel. Therein lay the biggest political bomb of the century. It would blow Los Angeles wide open, and the rats would come scurrying out. Tucker grinned. He'd be there, when they did come out, waiting with the biggest club he could find.

The throbbing pain behind Barker's eyes awakened him early that morning. He was getting used to hangovers, but this one was really a beaut. The lack of sleep and the liquid diet of the past few days had finally gotten to him. The chain-smoking hadn't helped either. He rolled over on his stomach and buried his face in the pillow. His hand reached down to the floor and brought up the empty Scotch bottle. Nothing could help him now but a stiff jolt.

Slowly, he sat up in the bed, afraid to move too fast, not wanting to tilt the delicate balance and black out. He sat like that for a few minutes, breathing through his mouth, getting used to the altitude. Then carefully he stood up and slowly made his way to the living room and the brown-and-tan leather upholstered bar. There was an open bottle of rye on the counter and he poured about four ounces into a water tumbler. He raised it to his lips and the smell of it made him gag, but he closed his eyes and swallowed it down quickly, the hundred-proof liquor burning his dry, parched throat, burning all the way down to his stomach. Then he stood gripping the edge of the bar as the tears ran down his cheeks, struggling for a breath of air.

He poured another four ounces into the tumbler and took it back with him into the bedroom. He stripped off the pajamas and went into the bathroom, stopping in front of the mirror cabinet to look at himself. What a frightful sight, he thought, pulling down on the skin under his eyes, scowling at the bloodshot eyes.

Ten minutes later he had shaved and showered, and felt a lot better. He came back into the bedroom, picked up the drink and sat on the edge of the bed, fingering the water tumbler, staring down at the amber liquid.

As drunk as he had been that night, he could still remember the plans he had made, and he reached down and picked up the scratch pad and smiled sadly at the scribbled figures. Things had looked a lot easier then. Now, in the cold light of day, his plan seemed preposterous. Nobody ever quit a hundred thousand a year job, he told himself, trying to ignore the real reason that made quitting impossible. "To hell with it," he shouted, without hearing the words, and gulped down the rest of the drink.

He jumped up and hurried out to the bar. This time he filled the tumbler right up to the brim, spilling some of it in his haste. Then he went out to the front door of the apartment and picked up the morning newspaper from the floor near the door, unaware of his nakedness and the startled gasp of a passing maid.

Retrieving the drink from the bar, he went back into the bedroom and sat on the bed. He opened the newspaper and stared at the headline, shocked almost into disbelief. For a blinding moment, a terrible rage swept through him and he cursed Alan Avery, pounding his fists into the soft mattress.

"Idiot," he cried. "Stupid idiot!"

Then he saw the light flashing, indicating that the telephone was ringing. He glared at it and reached for the tumbler of rye.

Marty Kahn sat behind his huge desk flanking the fieldstone fireplace in the den. He had made more than a dozen telephone calls since reading the newspaper account, and each call had added to his already highly manic state.

It was definite now. The grand jury would convene on Monday. And the word was out that Marty Kahn was to be its witness. Marty knew what that meant, and he wanted something done about it.

He picked up the telephone and again dialed Barker's number and waited, getting more impatient and irritated with each ring.

"Jesus H. Christ," he screamed as soon as he heard the receiver lifted at the other end. "Get the goddam lead out!"

"What is it now?" Barker demanded, his voice flat and annoyed.

"Have you seen the goddam papers?"

"Yes."

"Well! What are you doing about it?"

"Nothing."

"Yeah, well, you better do something goddam quick. I want action."

"On what?"

"Christ," Marty cried in disgust. "Where's your goddam

brain this morning?"

"Soaked in alcohol," Barker said, gulping down some of the rye.

"I'm in no mood for smart talk this morning," Kahn warned. "You get your ass over to City Hall and get my name scratched from that grand jury list. I can't stand no investigation now. Christ! Every son-of-a-bitching thing's going wrong. This is the worst stinking mess I've ever seen. You've got to do something, Doctor, and fast."

"What the hell can I do?"

"Get out there and spread some juice in the right places. Get the bastards interested in somebody else."

"Oh, fine," Barker said. "Is that all that's on your mind?"

"No. That teacher creep is really asking for it. He's the son of a bitch responsible for this goddam mess and I aim to get the bastard. He's gonna get hit."

"Don't do it," Barker shouted. "You leave Alan Avery alone. Understand?"

"Forget the bum. He's not your problem anymore. Leave it to Joe. You worry about that grand jury."

"I'm serious, Marty. I don't want Avery hurt."

"Listen, you son of a bitch, I haven't forgotten last night. Don't you start again this morning."

"God damn it, Marty. Be reasonable. Hurting Avery isn't going to help anything. It's a stupid, grandstand play that will really bring the heat on all of us. Let it alone for a while."

"You get to work on that grand jury and forget Avery. Don't give me no more trouble. I've taken all the goddam guff I'm gonna take from you. The next time you give me trouble I'm gonna bust your head for you."

Bryce finished the drink before speaking. "Marty, I don't like being threatened. If that's the way things are going to be between us, then I think it's time we called it quits."

"You're drunk," Kahn shouted. "Stinking drunk."

"I've never been more sober," Barker said, suddenly exhilarated by the decision that was now formed in the back of his mind.

"Get over here," Kahn said. "I want to talk to you."

"What about the grand jury?"

"Forget the grand jury. I want you here in exactly one hour. Understand?"

"Look, Marty, I've just told you I can't work this kind of a setup."

"One hour," Kahn shouted, and hung up.

After reading all the newspaper accounts, Ricca and Doto hurried out to Gracio's cottage at the Beverly Hills Hotel. Gracio and Nitta were having breakfast on the patio. Gracio stood up and shook hands with Joe, then nodded to Doto. Nitta patted Joe's knee when he sat down.

"Always glad to see one of the oldtimers," Nitta said, squinting his little eyes affectionately.

Ricca glanced at him and grinned.

Gracio was leaning back in the canvas chair. He wore dark blue linen Bermuda shorts and sandals. His muscular chest was bare and deeply tanned. With the dark sunglasses he now wore, he could have been any handsome movie star having breakfast before going out on location.

"It's too early to get emotional," he said, smiling pleasantly, showing his white teeth. "Well, Joe, things don't look too hot."

"I want that son of a bitch hit."

"Okay," Jimmy said. "I'll get you a contract."

"Right now," Ricca said. "Today!"

"Take it easy," Nitta said, patting Joe's knee. "Don't get in a sweat."

"That's right," Gracio said. "Look, maybe we can talk turkey to the bum."

"Shove that," Ricca said. "I'm all done footsing around. That son of a bitch's got to go."

"Calm down," Gracio said. "Remember, he's a teacher. A hit like that can mean a lot of trouble. Let's talk to him first. It's worth the try."

"I want a hit," Joe shouted, slamming his fist on the table, upsetting Gracio's coffee.

"I told you to calm down," Gracio said, the smile disappearing for a second. "This is a classy joint. Keep your voice down."

Suddenly, Ricca laughed a hard, harsh laugh. "Christ, Jimmy. Still worried about your goddam public appearance."

"No crap, now," Jimmy said. "Let's keep it down."

"Look, Jimmy," Ricca said. "Talk to the bum if you want. But I want a contract just in case. You know I want it available at a moment's notice."

"Good enough," Jimmy said. "I'm flying to Vegas at noon. I'll send Al down on the next flight late this afternoon."

"Al Rebos?"

"Yeah."

"God damn it, Jimmy, he's strictly explosives."

"Well, what's wrong with that? It's a different touch. And there's one thing about Al, you never have to worry about anything going wrong. He's the best in the business,"

"God damn, I'd like to do this hit myself."

"You just make sure you've got an airtight alibi. Have dinner with the mayor or something while it's happening."

"Don't worry about that end of it."

"Jack, bring the phone over here," Jimmy said, smiling, everything pleasant and charming again. "What's the bum's number?"

16.

Edie was determined to be bright and gay that Saturday morning. Alan was in the shower and she could hear the brisk downpour of water splashing against his body. He did look better this morning, not so pasty, and she even thought she had noticed a spot of color on his cheeks.

Like all Saturday and Sunday mornings she could remember, they had read the newspaper in bed, Alan taking the first half while she looked at the second, then exchanging halves. They both had read the headline story and the editorial without speaking about it. Edie had promised herself never to mention it again. She was going to be brave about everything except Alan's health. They had talked about it that morning and he had agreed to see a doctor after school on Monday.

She stood in the kitchen now, beating the eggs for the french toast. She always made french toast on Saturday morning, and it was usually a long process with her small frying pan, but they never minded the long leisurely breakfast. Sometimes, before she had gotten big with child, they had made love while waiting, and the toast burned, filling the house with smoke, and they had rushed about afterward, laughing, opening windows and fanning out the smoke.

Now she was too big, felt too awkward and she wished that the baby would come soon. She wanted to be small again, desirable, lovable. And every time she wished for the baby's arrival there was a sharp tug of fear at her heart.

She would make Alan happy today. She would do everything right. And above all, she would avoid any reference to those terrible gangsters. She would concentrate all her efforts on making him happy.

The day had taken on a mysterious significance. She had spent most of the night awake, watching Alan in his deep sleep, afraid to go to sleep herself because there was an urgency within her that she couldn't understand. She had stared at Alan's sleeping form with the intensity of a person determined to preserve an image, to press it upon the fabric of the mind forever.

She had felt like two persons. The one self that was planning for the future and wouldn't admit that life had come to an end. And the other self that recognized the ending and was trying to find something to preserve, something to give meaning to what had already ended.

She couldn't understand this kind of schizophrenic feeling, and she had never believed in premonition. But now as she stood in the kitchen with the sun streaming in, so bright and warm, she refused to think about it. Then she heard the water stop in the shower and she put the first french toast in the frying pan.

Alan looked at himself in the mirror as he wiped his thin body with the long turkish towel. He looked better this morning; maybe he even felt better. He wasn't sure. It was too early yet to tell. He threw the towel over the shower door and hurriedly slipped into boxer shorts. He came out of the steamy bathroom into the cool fresh air of the hallway and called out to Edie, "Be there in thirty seconds flat." Then he ran into the bedroom and slipped into freshly laundered faded blue denim pants, white T-shirt and blue denim gum-soled shoes.

"Here I am," he said, hurrying into the living room. "On time and starving."

"I've started the toast," she called.

"What's the mood this morning?" he asked, stopping before the record cabinet.

"Light and gay," she said, smiling from the open archway of the kitchen. "Fiedler and the Boston Pops."

"Feel gay, heh," he said, coming across the room to take her in his arms, "Did I tell you that I love you yet today?"

"No"

"I did, too."

"Don't remember." She was looking up at him, her eyes bright and smiling.

"Sure you do. You leaned over and said 'love you' and I said 'likewise.'"

"Tell me you love me," she said, curling her arms around his thin waist, her head leaning against his chest.

"I love you, little mother," he said, leaning down to kiss her, first on the forehead, slipping down to the nose then on her full lips. It had started out as just a kiss, but the urgency within her, the same urgency that had kept her awake half the night, reacted to the stimulus, and she brought her arms up around his neck and pressed his head down hard, her lips opening under the pressure, her tongue searching eagerly.

His hand slipped up under her breast and pressed, then moved over it, the fingers forming it to fit his hand. The other hand entered the back of the blouse and quickly unsnapped the brassiere, then he was pushing the blouse up and both his hands were over her bare breasts, feeling their warmth and full firmness.

She trembled against him, her eyes closed, breathing hard, and he picked her up and carried her into the bedroom and laid her down on the bed. He lay next to her, his head buried into the softness of her shoulder as his hands pulled the blouse and brassiere completely off.

Then his lips moved down to her breast and she reached over and pressed his head down hard against her.

"I love you," she said, her eyes closed.

"I know," he said, without looking up. "I know."

"Oh," she whimpered. "That's good. Oh...."

Merkle sat in a state of shock. It had been two hours since he had discovered the missing tapes, and he still couldn't believe it. He sat very erect, staring at the open partition door and the fat combination lock dangling there, undamaged. And the fear was there, eating at him, telling him that Marty Kahn would find out, and that when he did, it would be the end of Donald Merkle, the electronics wizard.

He sat there without moving, unable to decide on a course of action. He had to think, but he couldn't. So he just sat there, staring....

Captain Olin Martin, head of Intelligence Division, raised his hands up behind his head and leaned back in the gray steel leather-covered swivel chair, smiling. Tucker flipped off the playback switch on the tape machine and waited, expressionless, for Martin's comment.

"How many reels do you have?" Martin asked, flipping his feet up on top of the desk.

"Twenty-eight. Each runs two hours."

"Are they all as good as this?"

"I don't know. I haven't had time to listen to all of them."

Martin closed his eyes as his head went all the way back. "Not bad," he said. "Not bad at all. How did you get them?"

Tucker hesitated slightly and Martin quickly opened his eyes and came forward in the chair.

"What's the matter?"

"Nothing."

"Don't you trust me?"

"I don't know," Tucker said, staring hard at the captain.

"What are you doing here then?"

"I don't know. It was Johnson's idea. Maybe I'm in the wrong office."

"Oh, get off it. There are a few honest cops left on the force."

"Glad to hear it. What are you gonna do about it?"

"About what?"

"Finch."

Martin leaned back in the chair and smiled. "I've heard about that," he said.

"Well?"

"Sit down and cool off."

"Look," Tucker said, sitting down on a straight-backed chair, facing Martin. "We're not gonna get anywhere until I know what you plan to do about Finch."

"What do you want me to do?"

Tucker frowned, then slowly stood up and started to collect the reels of tape. "Forget it," he said, his voice heavy with sarcasm. "My mistake."

Martin's chair snapped forward and his feet hit the floor.

"Sit down, Sergeant," he said. "You're overstepping yourself."

Tucker looked up at him for a moment, then slowly and deliberately closed the lid to the recorder, sliding it off the desk.

"See you around, Captain," he said, and started for the door.

"God damn it," Martin shouted, coming around the desk and taking Tucker by the arm. "Why can't you get off that almighty high horse for a while and relax?"

"I don't have nothing to relax about."

"Listen," Martin said, pulling him back toward the chair. "Sit down and let's talk this thing out calmly and intelligently."

Tucker sat down, placing the machine at his feet, and patiently waited while Martin leaned back in his chair with his feet up on the desk top again.

"I know all about you, Tucker. I know about your trouble with Finch and I know how you feel about hoods you have to deal with every day. You see, it's part of my job. As head of Intelligence, I have to pass on the character and loyalty of every man on the force. Now, my other job is to fight organized crime. Your problem is right down the line. Understand?"

"There's no need to explain, Captain. All I'm interested in is Finch."

"Look," Martin said. "Finch will be taken care of in good time. First, I want my men to listen to all this tape and cull out the hot items. Then I want a written transcript of the whole thing. After that, we'll make out some cases."

"I've just given you a case."

"Not quite. But this with what I've already accumulated, plus what else there might be on those tapes, might give us an airtight case, and that's what I want. When you accuse a cop of being crooked, especially one with brass, you better be goddam sure of your footing."

"You've got a file on Finch?"

"Sure. I've got a file on you, too."

"Yeah. Anything there about why I was transferred to patrol?"

Martin smiled and reached over and flipped the intercom switch. "Bring me the Tucker file," he said, and leaned back again, studying Tucker through half-closed lids.

Tucker's face was expressionless as he stared back at Martin. Neither man moved or talked as the uniformed policeman placed the file before Martin and went out. Martin swung his feet off the desk and came forward in the chair. He opened the manila folder and fingered through the file.

"Take a look at this," he said, tossing some papers toward Tucker.

At first Tucker didn't recognize it. It was printed on photographic paper and was slightly bigger than the original handwritten report he had submitted to Finch. But it was the same report, and this surprised him. He quickly looked up at Martin, his dark eyes puzzled.

"See," Martin said, smiling smugly. "We're not all so stupid."

"How did you get this?"

Martin laughed. "Never mind. Now, do we work together or do I have to get tough?"

"Tell me, Captain," Tucker said. "How long were you gonna wait before doing anything about this?"

"I have two ways of working. Normally when I see a report come through—for instance, on a bookie drop—I file it. The next report that comes in on that same drop is a different story. I call up the responsible officer and I lay it on the line. 'Are you gonna close him up, or do you want me to do it, or shall we do it together.' That's the procedure I follow when I think the officer is straight, but a little lax or careless. If I suspect the worst, I just sit tight and wait while my boys go out and work up a case. An airtight case. Finch is that kind of case. Understand?"

"Okay," Tucker said, standing up. "Come on. I'll take you to the bug."

The door to Merkle's shop was locked when they arrived. They banged on the door for a while, then Tucker took out his pick and went to work on the lock while Martin leaned against the dirty plate-glass window, softly whistling.

"Is this the way you got in the first time?" Martin asked.

"Yeah. That's the way."

"Pretty lucky."

"I suppose."

"There's no supposing. What if there hadn't been any

bug and you had been caught?"

"It was the chance I took."

"Yeah. That's what I mean. Pretty lucky."

The door swung open and Tucker went in with Martin right behind him.

"Merkle!" Tucker called as he hurried to the back of the shop. The door to the toilet was closed and Tucker went up to it and turned the knob. It was locked.

"Merkle, are you in there? This is Sergeant Tucker. Come on out of there."

Slowly the door opened and Merkle's head came peering out cautiously, his eyes wild with fear as he looked at the two officers.

"Whatta you want?" he asked, without leaving the security of the toilet.

"Come out here," Tucker said, "We want to talk to you."

"Go on and talk," he said. "I'm listening."

Tucker jumped forward and slammed his foot against the door, as he grabbed Merkle by the arm and pulled him out into the room.

"Into the bug room," he said, coming up behind the little man.

"Don't push me around," Merkle whined. "I've got connections downtown."

"Yeah," Tucker said. "I know. You're gonna call Lieutenant Finch."

"That's right," Merkle said. "He'll take care of you guys."

"Get in there," Tucker said, almost lifting him off his feet as he pushed him toward the opened partition door. "Tell the captain here how it works," he said, pointing at the three tape recorders.

"You're the guy who broke in here last night," Merkle screamed, finally realizing what had happened. "I'm gonna sue you for breaking in. That's what I'm gonna do. You wait and see."

"Go ahead and sue," Tucker said. "It will make Marty Kahn mighty happy to hear those tapes played in court."

"No," Merkle cried, backing away. "You're not gonna tell him. He'll kill me. You don't know him. He'll kill me for sure."

"Aw, shut up," Martin said, "before I kill you myself."

Merkle's teeth clicked together, his small eyes puzzled and afraid.

"Now," Tucker said. "Explain it to the captain."

Merkle slowly moved up to the machine and stared at them without speaking.

"Well!"

"This one here is connected to Kahn's living room," he said, pointing at the first one in the row. "The next one is for the den. And the third one was a phone tap at Marsha's place."

"What do you mean was?" Martin asked.

"I've disconnected it."

"Why?"

"Kahn was getting wise."

"Connect it again," Martin said.

"No," Merkle said. "I can't do that."

"Sure you can."

"No, no, no."

"I wouldn't be so positive if I were you," Martin said.

"I can't take the chance."

"Why aren't the others on?"

"I turned them off yesterday."

"Well, well, now," Martin said. "We'll have to see about that."

"I don't want nothing to do with it. I want to get out of town for a while."

"Later," Martin said. "First, I want all these machines

connected and running. Understand?"

"What about me?" Merkle cried. "You've got to protect me."

"Sure," Martin said. "You worry too much."

"If he finds out he'll kill me."

"You should have thought of that before," Tucker said.

"I know," Merkle said. "God, how I know that now. I just about went crazy this morning. You've got to protect me. That guy will blow my brains out without blinking an eye."

"Sure," Martin said. "We'll protect you. Don't worry."

"I want a bodyguard twenty-four hours a day."

"Sure," Martin said. "But first, get them things working. Then we'll talk about protection."

"I can't fix the phone tap. I've destroyed the lines."

"Don't give me any trouble. Get it connected."

"I'll have to get into the phone line again."

"Get into it."

"Not in the daytime."

"Get going and stop worrying."

"Okay," Merkle said. "But don't forget about the protection. I'm gonna need it. Real bad."

Edie stood in the middle of the kitchen, waving the newspaper, while Alan hurriedly opened all the windows. The french toast had burned again, and the smoke filled the small apartment with its sweet, pungent odor.

The phone rang and Edie picked it up, laughing a little as she answered it.

"Mrs. Avery?"

"Yes."

"You wanta keep your husband alive, lady?"

"Who is this?" Edie asked, fear suddenly suffocating her.

"Get him on the line. I wanta talk to him."

Alan had stopped fanning the smoke and stood watching her. Whatever it was, he knew it was bad. She turned a pale, frightened face to him, her lips trembling, her whole body hunched over as she held out the phone.

"Yes," Alan said into the receiver, his eyes on Edie.

"Avery, I've got a message for you. And you better listen real close. I'm gonna speak man to man, see. You've been real stupid getting mixed up in something that don't concern you ..."

"Who is this?" Alan interrupted.

"Never mind. Just listen ..."

"I don't want to listen to that kind of talk."

"You son of a bitch, you better listen. I'm giving you twenty-four hours to change your goddam story to the goddam cops."

"I'm going to hang up," Alan said.

"You hang up that damn phone, Jack, and I'll be there in person in fifteen minutes flat and you'll be one sorry son of a bitch."

"Who are you?"

"I'm just the guy that's gonna blow your head off, that's who I am, you stupid son of a bitch. Who do you think you're dealing with, anyway. I'm gonna tell you something, you bastard. No son of a bitching bum ever put the heat on Joe Ricca and lived to tell about it. Now, you don't have to take my word for it. Just check Joe's news clippings. You'll find out goddam quick enough, and don't think the cops are gonna help you, either. Remember. Twenty-four hours. You change your story or I'll blow your head right off your shoulders." And the line went dead.

Alan stood with the dead phone in his hand, his thin face, pale and pinched, his gray eyes dark and staring vacantly at the black instrument in his hand. Then he looked up and saw Edie's frightened eyes watching him, and he fought for control, knowing that he would need all the strength he could muster. He replaced the receiver and went to Edie, taking her in his arms, petting her gently on the shoulder, feeling her trembling.

"Don't worry," he said. "I'll call Lieutenant Johnson. Everything will be all right. You wait and see. There's nothing to worry about."

She waited to speak, waited until she had full control of herself, until she knew that her voice would not betray her.

"See Bryce Barker," she said, without looking up, her face still pressed against his chest. "Maybe he can help us."

"I don't think I should," he said.

"Please, Alan, see him right away."

"All right, Edie," he said. "I'll go there just as soon as I call Lieutenant Johnson."

17.

Marty Kahn stood with his back to the swimming pool and glared at the three men before him as he slammed his hard fist into the palm of his hand.

"After all I've done for that bastard," he shouted. "All the goddam loot I've given him. Christ, I've made him a rich man, and that's the goddam thanks I get. Well, we'll see. We'll goddam well see. I'm not crapping, either. I'm gonna fix his wagon. You wait and see. The lousy deaf son of a bitch."

"What're you waiting for?" Ricca asked. "Send Doto to get him. I'll take care of that wise mouthpiece for you. I always wanted to take a poke at that bastard. He thinks he's God."

"Never mind," Kahn said. "I'm gonna teach him a lesson. That's for goddam sure. He's been with me ten years, and everything has been real silk until this week. I think it's that teacher."

"Don't worry about that bum," Joe said. "Al Rebos is gonna take care of him."

"Oh, Jesus!" Kahn cried. "Not that crazy bastard?"

"What's wrong?"

"He's gonna blow him up. A thing like that can cause real trouble. Christ, man. He's a teacher, you know. Make a lot of people mad. The fuzz will really be breathing down our necks."

"Stow the fuzz. We'll have perfect alibis."

"We better. And that's no goddam bull."

Just then the Mexican houseboy came running out of the house with the telephone in his hand, uncoiling the long cord behind him.

"Very important," he said, handing the phone to Marty.

"Okay," Marty said. "Beat it." And he waited until the boy had disappeared inside the house before speaking into the receiver.

"Yeah," he said. "This is Kahn."

Then he listened, and his eyes grew larger and larger, and he began to pace up and down, his teeth flashing out to bite into the thick lower lip, perspiration breaking out of his pudgy, red face. Then, in a fit of blind rage, he flung the telephone across the patio and stood there, crouched low, his breathing hard and rapid, his large eyes shifting wildly, his feet stamping up and down like a child throwing a tantrum. Then he ran forward and kicked the telephone, screaming in pain as his bare toes struck the heavy base. He hobbled around on one foot as he came back to the three men who sat without expression on their hard faces.

"I want Merkle dead. Understand. Dead! Right now!"

"What's up?" Ricca asked.

"The son of a bitch bugged this house, and the cops

have all the tapes. I want him dead! Today."

Ricca stood up and nodded to Doto and Little Abner. "Get over to Barker's place and pick him up. You, Axe, bring him back here in his fancy car. And you, Little Abner, keep the Cad and get down to Merkle's place and get him. Understand? You get him even if it takes you all day and all night. Now, get going."

"Don't you come back here until you get him," Kahn shouted, as the two men hurried away. "I want that bastard dead! Dead, dead, dead!"

Ricca looked at Kahn and smiled. "We'll take care of Barker while we're at it."

"Yeah, yeah," Kahn said, pacing nervously before the pool. "We've got to get that bastard on the ball."

"Leave him to me," Ricca said. "I'll take care of everything."

Alan Avery took a cab to Bryce Barker's apartment on Wilshire in Westwood. It was a twelve-story snow-white building with plenty of class. There was a wide circular drive leading to the front entrance, and a doorman in a two-toned green outfit with epaulets stepped smartly forward and smiled as he opened the cab door.

"Welcome to Whiteside Manor," he said.

Alan nodded to him, paid the cabby, and started for the entrance. The doorman was now holding the huge plate-glass door open, still smiling. Alan stepped into the lobby and glanced around him, suddenly awe struck by the lavish simplicity of the modern decor.

The desk clerk told him Barker's room number and Alan rode the elevator to the tenth floor. He pressed the doorbell and heard the melodious sound of chimes. A moment later, the door flew open and a blue-eyed, black-haired girl with a skin as white as the outside of the building was standing there, bubbling with excitement.

"Where have you ..." And the bubble suddenly burst. "Oh, I'm sorry," she said, embarrassed.

"I'm looking for Mr. Barker," he said.

"Mr. Barker is out at the moment."

"May I wait for him? I'm Alan Avery."

"Why, yes, come in," Diane said, recognizing the name from the newspapers. "I'm sure Mr. Barker will be most pleased to see you."

Alan followed her into the large living room with the huge windows overlooking the city and the thick white carpet and green-and-gray tile fireplace. The furniture was late contemporary, imported from Sweden. There were excellent reproductions of modern paintings on the light gray walls and a huge original abstract hung over the fireplace.

"Can I get you a drink?" Diane asked, sitting on the long, low circular sofa facing the fireplace. She looked at him and smiled.

"No thank you," Alan said, still standing, feeling uneasy in the splendor of the room, and the cool charm of the beautiful dark-haired girl.

"Please sit down, Mr. Avery," she said, indicating a white leather chair between the sofa and fireplace. Alan sat down in the low chair and crossed his long legs, his knees coming up almost as high as his face.

"I'm a friend of Mr. Barker," she found herself saying without knowing why. "I'm also waiting to see him."

"Yes. I see," Alan said, and tried to smile, but it was no use. He had never felt less like smiling in his whole life. And he sat there, hearing the black-haired, white-faced girl's voice, but was unable to concentrate on the words. He thought of Edie and how brave she had looked when he had left, how brave that small, fragile face had been as he had leaned down to kiss the cold, trembling lips. Things had happened so quickly. Two days ago, at this time, he was standing in a classroom at Hollywood High School and everything had been normal. He was just Alan Avery, teacher, husband, father-to-be.

Then suddenly everything had changed. He was the new Alan Avery. The man who had fingered the mob. The man with his picture on the front page of the newspaper. The fearless idealist who had taken a stand against murderers. The man most likely to have his head blown off. And that part of it, when he had first heard the man's voice on the telephone, had frightened him at first. Then the fear had been replaced by indignation, then anger, and finally back to fear, the whole cycle repeating itself, time and time again. He could still hear that gruff voice, spitting out the obscenities, the violence raw and naked in the angry threat. There was no doubt in Alan's mind that the man had meant every word he had spoken. Alan knew that his safety depended on the skill of the police. He had no hopes that Barker could or would help him. He was doing this to please Edie.

Diane realized that Alan wasn't listening and stopped talking. She leaned back in the soft cushions, watching him through half-closed lids, wondering what made a man that was so tall and skinny, so brave and stupid. And it made her feel good and warm inside. Proud that there were men like that left in the world.

Diane heard the key in the lock and jumped off the sofa and ran toward the opening door, throwing herself into Barker's arms. Barker smiled crookedly and slapped her across the buttocks. She pulled back, embarrassed, knowing that Alan was watching. Barker lurched forward, almost falling, his arms reaching out for her, grinning foolishly.

"Whatsa matter," he asked, "don't you wanta play?"

"Mr. Alan Avery is here to see you," she said, still backing away, realizing how drunk he really was.

"Who?"

"Mr. Alan Avery."

"I'll be damned," he said, lurching into the room. "Alan, for Christ's sake, what are you doing in this den of iniquity?"

Alan stood up and shook hands. "I'd like to talk to you."

"Wait a minute," Barker said. "I've got some real news for both of you. Cause you know you're both my best friends. And I want you two to be the first to know."

He stopped and grinned at both of them.

"I've quit," he declared, waving his arms like an umpire calling a runner safe at second. "I'm all done being somebody's slave. This is emancipation day for Bryce Barker."

Diane slowly sat down and stared up at him, her eyes incredulous. "You don't mean it!" she said. "You can't possibly mean it!"

"Oh, yes, I do," he said. "I told him to go take a running dive for himself. Just like that." Barker grinned and passed his hand over his eyes. "Well, maybe not like that. But I told him. I don't remember exactly what I said. But whatever it was, I said it. What do you think of that, Mr. Alan Avery?"

"That's fine," Alan said, not knowing what else he could say.

"I was just out trying to sell the old hot-rod. Man, what a town this is. Everybody sells. Nobody buys. Well, by God, I'll fix them. I'm gonna give it to you, Alan. You'll be the only teacher in the whole Los Angeles school system driving a twenty-thousand-dollar jalopy. How do you like that, pal?"

"Thanks," Alan said, "but I couldn't accept it."

"Why not? We're old friends, aren't we? Hell, we went to school together. Come on, now. Don't be like that. I want you to have it. I insist."

"I can't accept it," Alan said. "I appreciate your generous offer, but it's completely impossible."

"Well," Diane said. "If that's the case, how about me? Ask me, why don't you?"

"What'd you want it for?"

"So I can give it back to you tomorrow when you sober up."

Barker scowled at her, then turned to Alan. "Am I drunk? Do I look drunk to you? Goddam women are all alike. Take a drink and you're a goddam lush. Well, I'm gonna tell you something, my pretty, blue-eyed baby. I'm shoving off. Not only out of this stinking smog sewer, but out of the country completely. I'm going to Switzerland, and I'm leaving as soon as I get my passport."

"What about me?" Diane asked, fear in her blue eyes.

"Well, what about you?"

"Thanks," she said, jumping up. "Thanks for the buggy ride." And she spun around, but he reached over and caught her.

"Let me go," she cried, the tears welling up in her eyes.

"How long will it take you to get a passport?" he asked.

The tears stopped. Her whole face lighted up, then crumbled as she threw herself into his arms and cried, the tears flowing down her cheeks, her eyes bright and shining, as she pressed herself against him in a moment of wild joy.

Barker glanced at Alan and winked as his hand reached down and patted her on the buttocks. She didn't object this time, but just pressed harder against him.

"I think I better go," Alan said.

"Wait," Barker said. "What's on your mind?"

"Nothing of importance," Alan said.

"Now," Barker said, "you didn't come here for nothing."

"I've changed my mind," Alan said, and hurried to the door.

"Okay," Barker said. "I'll give you a ring before I leave."

"Good luck," Alan said, going out and closing the door softly behind him.

Barker had just time for another drink before Doto and Little Abner arrived. He sat on the sofa with Diane and they made plans.

Two years, at least, in the Swiss Alps. It seemed too good to be true. And she thought of Catherine in *Farewell to Arms*, and the great love she had enjoyed in Switzerland.

"Let's go to Montreux," she said.

And he laughed and asked why. And she laughed and told him how she had always envied Catherine, and he remembered and said he was not Henry.

"But you could grow a beard," she said, "and I could get pregnant. And we'll live in a house in Montreux and we'll take long walks in the deep snow and stop at the inn for hot red wine with spices and lemon in it. Then we'll walk through the woods on our way back home and make love in the white snow and the foxes will come out of their holes to watch. It will be great fun and you'll have a splendid beard, and I'll be oh so big in the belly. At night you can lie with your head floating on top of it, and it will be as soft as foam rubber, and you can listen to what the little bastard is doing in there while I'm sleeping."

Barker laughed and patted her stomach, and did his own dreaming. He, too, had a special image of Switzerland. To him it was a country of white mountains and long ski tows, and he saw himself sweeping down the white slopes, graceful as a bird, twisting and turning, the snow a white spray. There were the evenings, too. Sitting before an open fire, reading, Diane sitting across from him, knitting, looking up every now and then to smile happily. It was a fine dream; and it ended with the sound of the door chimes.

Barker knew when he saw Doto and Little Abner standing in the opened doorway that there was going to be trouble. And he knew that it was futile of him to refuse to do as they demanded. It would mean only more trouble, and perhaps trouble for Diane, which he wanted to avoid at all cost.

Diane pleaded with him not to go. But he told her it was only fair that he see Marty and break everything off like a man, face to face.

"Start packing," he said, smiling at her from the open door. "We're practically on our way."

Barker drove the Ferrari to Kahn's place with Doto sitting next to him, grinning morosely. Barker had decided upon a plan of action. It would be ridiculous for him to tell Kahn he was quitting. The best thing would be to go along with Kahn, then make his break as soon as he got the passport. It would have to be done with the utmost secrecy. He was sorry now that he had spouted off on the telephone that morning. Why couldn't he have used his head and played it smart? Well, maybe it wasn't too late. Sooner or later, Kahn would stop talking and listen to him. Then he could smooth everything over. Tell Kahn he was drunk and didn't mean a word of it. Then he thought about the trip to Switzerland and smiled.

"Ever been to Europe?" he asked Doto, as he swung the car through the opened gates and came to a stop before the four-car garage.

"Nope," Doto said. "Never had no time for that."

"Too bad," Barker said. "You ought to go there sometime. Fine country. Especially Switzerland."

"Sure, sure," Doto said, following Barker up the walk. They walked into the entrance hall and into the empty living room. Barker stopped and looked around. "Where's everybody?" he asked.

"In the den," Doto said.

Barker heard the loud music coming from the den and hurried into the room. Just as he stepped through the open door, Ricca came up from behind and flipped a rope over his head, bringing it up tight around his neck. Barker struck out blindly, swinging his arms in a wide arc, but Ricca was already applying pressure to the rope and Barker felt the rope cut into his throat, choking him. He saw Kahn standing before the big desk, watching, his eyes big and luminous. Then Doto was holding his feet and he tried to struggle as Ricca brought the rope around again for a double loop. Then he felt himself falling to the floor, his feet up in the air, as Doto pressed his knees back against his chest. He stopped struggling for a moment, unable to understand what was happening to him. He could feel the wild pounding of his heart as he watched the blurred figures of Ricca and Doto move quickly above him.

Then before he realized it, he was tied up like a little ball with his head pushed down on his chest, his hands folded in between, the rope coming down from this neck to under his feet. He couldn't move without tightening the rope around his throat. He remembered having heard the boys talk about this kind of roping. It had been a specialty of Murder Inc., and it was usually followed by an icepick in the back a few dozen times. He tried to move. It was hopeless. He couldn't even breathe, and when he tried to raise his head to open his throat, the rope cut in deeper against his windpipe.

"Just like the old days," Doto said, laughing as he wiped the perspiration from his wet face.

"Getting a little rusty," Ricca said. "We used to pull it off in half the time."

Marty came forward and stood looking down at Barker. "Well, Doctor," he said. "Feel like quitting now?"

There was a loud hum in Barker's ears and he felt the waves of nausea sweeping through him, and he tried to ignore them, but they welled up in his burning throat, and he felt bubbles coming out of his mouth and dripping on the carpet. He knew then he was going to die. He knew that he would never see Switzerland. Never hold or touch Diane again. And he remembered his father, saw him standing on the steeple, his pants legs flapping in the wind, his face old and gray, his eyes sad, faded with age. Then he was falling through space, falling silently toward the screaming crowd below, his body turning over and over, his arms flailing the air like a fledgling trying to take flight.

Then the retching was really upon him, and the dry heaves shook his body, bringing the hard rope up against his throat like a knife, and his lungs gasped for air, bursting with the need of it, and he felt the buzz in his ears grow louder and louder, until finally it exploded like a bomb in his head.

"What the hell is that?" Marty shouted, pointing at Barker's mouth.

"Blood," Ricca said. "What the hell did you think it was?"

"Get something under him. I don't want this goddam carpet stained."

Doto took the newspaper off the desk and placed it under Barker's head. "He's out," he said.

"Jesus H. Christ." Kahn said. "I wanted to talk to him."

"He'll be all right later," Ricca said, winking at Doto.

"Move him over there," Kahn said, "Behind the bar. I'll talk to him later."

"Sure," Ricca said. "There's plenty of time. Oh, by the way, did Marie fix up the party?"

"I don't like it," Kahn said. "We should leave that teacher alone for now."

"Stop worrying. The party is a perfect alibi."

"Yeah, I know," Kahn said. "But I still don't like it."

When Little Abner left Doto and Barker in front of the Whiteside Manor, he drove directly to Merkle's shop on Santa Monica Boulevard. He drove slowly past the shop at least a dozen times, trying to peer through the dirty plate-glass window. It was bright sunshine outdoors and dark inside the poorly lighted store, making it almost impossible for Little Abner to see anything. He drove down the street a block and parked the car, then walked back on the other side of the street. There was a sidewalk telephone booth almost directly across the street from Merkle's shop and Little Abner squeezed his huge body into the booth and sat down.

After a while he saw Merkle come to the front door and peer out. He looked up and down the street then spat on the sidewalk and went back inside.

Little Abner was sure he had seen the shadow of another man in the back of the shop and he waited now to verify this before deciding on what to do. This was a particularly special job for Little Abner. It was his first assignment on his own and he was determined to make good. He would be extremely careful and plan everything down to the finest detail. Marty would be proud of him. Real proud. He scratched his head and tried to think.

18.

Al Rebos arrived from Las Vegas on the four o'clock flight. He sat looking out the small window as the plane came to a stop at the end of the runway and turned around, heading toward the ramp.

He smiled wistfully and patted his hair carefully back in place. His hair was thin on top and he had let the sides grow long, then parted the long hairs over the top in an effort to cover the bald spot, giving him an old-fashioned appearance. His face was thin and his eyes looked enormous behind the thick-lensed glasses. He had a nervous twitch at the right side of his mouth that ran all the way up to his eye, making his eye blink every time the muscles contracted.

Al Rebos was a young man of many afflictions. Besides the twitch and myopic eyesight, he had a serious speech impediment, a lisp that had slowly developed into stutter. Through the years his many physical defects had contributed to his mental defects. Al Rebos had lived with a feeling of inferiority for twenty-six years, and during those years he had learned to hate the human race. He had no friends and he trusted no one. He worked quickly and efficiently, without fanfare, and from a long distance,

He had never killed with a knife or a gun, and would shudder at the very thought of it. His first job had been with explosives when he was only seventeen.

He had placed a bomb in the car of his adoptive uncle, who had raised Al since the age of twelve. Al was at the movies when the bomb went off and by the time he got home the body had been removed to the city morgue. Al never saw the mangled body and to him his uncle had just died. His killing had been remote and impersonal. Al had never felt responsible for his uncle's death.

Since then he had placed dozens of bombs in all kinds of places and he had killed dozens of people. He didn't really know how many; Al Rebos was not one to keep count. Once the bomb was placed, he went away and that was the end of it. He never read the newspaper account of it, never thought about it again.

The plane came to a stop and the stewardess stood by the opened door, smiling at the departing passengers. Al picked up his briefcase from the floor at his feet and meekly made his way down the narrow aisle.

"Thank you. Hope you enjoyed your trip," the stewardess said as Al went by with his head down.

He found the black Ford sedan parked in front of the Administration Building. The door was unlocked and the keys were in the ignition switch. He slipped into the car and placed the large briefcase on the seat next to him.

He drove with his eye on the rear-view mirror, watching the big black Cadillac behind him. He turned up a side street and the Cadillac followed. Al repeated the procedure for a number of turns, then brought the Ford to a stop in front of a fenced-in vacant lot. He turned the ignition off, pulled up the emergency brake, examined his hair in the rear-view mirror, patted a few stray long hairs back into place, his eye suddenly blinking as the right side of his face collapsed in a twitch. He always hated to see the twitch and he quickly turned away from the mirror, repulsed by the contorting muscles.

The briefcase was tucked securely under his arm when he stepped out of the Ford and walked back to the Cadillac. Ricca saw him coming and nudged Doto.

"Christ! He's even uglier than you," he said, laughing.

Doto glanced at Ricca, his fat greasy face twisted in anguish. "Well, I should hope so. He's the ugliest bastard alive."

Al Rebos came up to the window on the driver's side and looked at Ricca, without speaking.

"How's everything in Vegas?" Ricca said.

Al nodded and shrugged his shoulders.

"Well, here's the contract. This is a picture of the bum with his name and address on the back. I want him to be hit tonight."

"Wa-wa-wait a-a-a m-minute!" He stopped and tried to get control of himself. "G-G-G-Gra-c-c-cio s-s-said t-t-to-m-m-morr-row."

"Tonight," Ricca said.

"I-I-I d-d-don't k-k-know. G-g-g-got ca-ca-case th-the j-j-j-joint."

"Look," Ricca said. "If you can't do it tonight. Forget it. Go back to Vegas. I'll do the job myself."

"N-n-now wa-wa-wait a-a-a-a s-s-sec."

"I mean it," Ricca said. "It's tonight. I don't give a good goddam what Jimmy told you. I'm running this deal. Understand?"

"O-o-o-o-k-kay," he said, his eyes bulging out every time he spoke.

"Need any help? Crash car? Anything at all?"

"N-n-no."

"Call me up at Kahn's when it's all set up. But remember I want it done between eight and one tonight. We're gonna have a little party at Kahn's to set up the alibi."

"Okay," he said, his enormous eyes pleased that he had spoken a complete word without stuttering.

Edie sat at the dining table, watching Alan, her food untouched. Alan looked at her and smiled, a warm, gentle, understanding smile. He put his fork down and took a sip of hot tea.

"I'm not hungry either," he said, looking down at her plate.

"How about a little walk later on? We need some fresh air."

"Fine," she said, trying to smile. "I'd like that very much."

"Look, Edie," he said. "I know what you're thinking. And I'm sorry."

"I haven't said a word," she said. "You don't have to explain. I understand."

"Do you really understand? Look, Edie, I'm not trying to be a hero. I'm not even brave. I'm scared, too, but not scared enough to sacrifice my self-respect. I realize there are thousands of people dominated by gangsters. I know that some people think it's a lot easier just to pay the gangster and stay out of trouble. They pay tribute to gangsters all their lives. I know all that, Edie, but I can't understand how these people can willingly makes slaves of themselves in a free country. They might just as well be living under the worst kind of dictatorship. There's no difference. They live in fear all their lives, bowing to corruption and violence, not knowing from day to day what the gangsters will do to them."

He stopped and looked at her, his hand reaching out to touch hers.

"You know, Edie," he said, "this is the first time I've ever had to fight for my freedom. Even in the war it was easy for me. I spent the whole four years in the States. Never saw any action. Never had to take the slightest risk. Now, for the first time in my life, I have to do something to earn this privilege. Now I have to fight, and I'm going to the only way I know—with the truth and with the courage to say it. And I won't be deterred by threats or by violence itself."

Edie was out of her chair and running to him. He stood up and took her in his arms, and together they walked over to the sofa and sat down, Edie on his lap, her head curled on his shoulder, her face buried in his neck.

"I love you so much," she whispered, kissing his neck.

"And I love you," he said, patting her hip. "And I'm glad I married you. Very glad."

There was a knock at the door and Alan gently pushed Edie off his lap and went to the door. The man standing in the doorway was small and his eyes were enormous as he looked up at Alan. There was a quick flurry of twitches that caved in the right side of his face, making his eye wink grotesquely, as he tried to speak.

"Th-t-t-th-t-t—" His eyes bulged out, staring intensely, his free hand waving before his face, trying to help the struggling sound. His other hand held a large briefcase.

"Can I help you?" Alan said, familiar with the stuttering problem after years of teaching.

The little man shook his head and backed away, going down the outdoor staircase. Alan watched him until he had reached the sidewalk and slipped into a black Ford sedan waiting at the curb. He heard the sound of the engine, then the headlights came on and the car disappeared down the street.

Tucker sliced a piece of the thick steak and speared it into his mouth. It tasted good, but not half as good as what Martin had told him. That had been really tasty. Tucker was glad he had seen Martin. He was the right man, all right. He would take care of Finch. He had already agreed to turn over all the tapes to the grand jury when it convened on Monday. "What if the D.A. objects?" Tucker had asked. "Don't worry about it," Martin had replied. "I know a few big shots myself. I don't hold this rank for nothing."

That was the kind of a cop Tucker liked. Here was a cop who was out to do his duty in spite of the crazy laws and people standing in the way. Martin had not gone all to pieces when Tucker had told him about breaking into Merkle's shop. And he hadn't been concerned about whether the bugs constituted an invasion of privacy. His job as a cop was to put Marty Kahn behind bars, and the only way to do that was to get him any way you could. Everybody knew that Kahn and Ricca were crooks and killers, and yet they all worried about civil rights and due process of the law. To hell with that, Tucker thought. Only a fool fought fair in a dirty fight. And any cop who tried to fight fair when fighting gangsters and murderers was the biggest, deadest fool of all. The only good gangster, the only reformed one, was a dead one.

Tucker took another bite and looked up to see Lieutenant Johnson sitting down next to him at the table. Johnson's dull eyes followed the thick slice of steak on its way up into Tucker's mouth. He took out a cigarette and lighted it, letting the smoke just drift out of his mouth in thick layers. Then impatiently he blew it all away.

"Was up at Merkle's place. Interesting. Very interesting," he said.

"I thought so," Tucker said, leaning over the steaming coffee to sip a little. "Oughtta put away a few characters where they belong."

"Could be," Johnson said.

"What'd you mean, could be?"

"Just that. I've seen a lot of good things blow right up into fat zeros. So could this."

"I don't think so," Tucker said.

"Let's hope not," Johnson said.

"Martin said he was gonna see to it."

"Well, you've got yourself a good man there, all right. If anybody can do it, he can. Olin's a good cop. And so are you, Ernie. The two of you should turn the trick. Good luck, anyway."

"Thanks," Tucker said, proud that Johnson thought

well of him. "We're gonna do our best. But what brings you here?"

"Well," Johnson said. "I just thought you might be interested to know that somebody telephoned Alan Avery today and threatened his life."

Tucker stopped eating and stared at Johnson. "On the level? Not a crackpot or anything like that?"

"Seems straight enough. Gave Avery twenty-four hours to change his story. Otherwise they threatened to blow his head off."

"I'm not surprised."

"I know," Johnson said. "I was expecting it. It certainly punches a fat hole in Scipio's balloon."

Tucker said, annoyed, "You never believed that little pimp, did you?"

"Look," Johnson said. "I don't like the thought of losing that witness."

"I don't either."

"I know that. That's why I'm gonna ask you to take over the assignment of protecting him. I'll get you transferred to Homicide. Give you all the men you need for the job. I'd like you to supervise it."

"Well, I'll be," Tucker laughed. "The lieutenant has a heart, after all."

"None of that, now," Johnson said, his face hardening.

"Okay," Tucker said. "But how about tonight?"

"No need to worry about tonight. They gave him twenty-four hours. They're hoping to scare him. But between you and me, I don't think they will. There's a lot of strength in that boy."

"Let's hope so," Tucker said, picking up his fork again.

"Will you take the assignment?"

"My pleasure. I think I'll drop over there tonight."

Martin stood in the small partitioned room and watched

the uniformed police technician as he worked the dials on the tape recorder. Merkle stood alongside the officer, fidgeting nervously, his small eyes watching every movement.

"What the hell's all this goddam music?" Martin asked.

"They're wise to the bug," the officer said. They're jamming it with the radio. If that's the case, we're not gonna get anything worth a damn on this setup from here on in."

"Can you make out anything at all?"

"They're having a party, I think. There's a lot of noise in the background. People talking and laughing. I thought I caught Cliff Spar's name a while ago. You know, the actor."

"Could be," Martin said. "He's one of them stupid actors who thinks it's smart to chum around with hoodlums."

"That's right," Merkle said. "He's there all the time."

"Well, one of these days he's gonna discover it's not so clever to buddy up with rats. But those characters never learn until it's too late."

"I wonder what the occasion is?" the officer asked. "They certainly don't have nothing to celebrate about. That's for damn sure."

"Maybe it's a last fling," Martin grinned.

Alan and Edie were just leaving for their walk when Tucker arrived. They met outside on the staircase. Tucker tipped his hat when introduced to Edie.

"Going anywhere in particular?" he asked.

"No, just for a walk," Alan said. "Thought we'd get a little fresh air."

"How about a ride?" Tucker asked, smiling up at Edie.

Alan looked at Edie and she nodded. "Okay," he said. "It's a ride then."

They drove in silence at first, the three of them sitting in the front seat, Edie in the middle.

"Don't you own a car?" Tucker asked.

"We used to," Alan said. "But with the baby coming and everything we decided to sell it. Too expensive. Actually, we didn't really need it. I ride to school with a friend. There's no garage with the apartment and the car stayed on the street all the time. We used it only on weekends to go to the beach and shopping."

"Teachers are like policemen. They feed at the public trough."

"Well," Alan said. "It's not too bad. We get enough to get by. And that's certainly more than a lot of people get. I'm satisfied."

"I don't know about that," Tucker said. "In Los Angeles everybody has at least one car. Most of them have two. It's like bathrooms. Even the smallest tract homes have two bathrooms now, and some even have two and a half." He looked at Edie and grinned. "Gosh, I remember the days when you were lucky to have a toilet. You took your bath in a wash basin every Saturday night. Now, you know, it's a shower every morning and night. The whole family takes a shower at the same time. This must be the cleanest town in the world."

Edie laughed heartily and Alan was happy. "I used to take a bath in an old washtub right in the middle of the kitchen," Alan said. "It used to be pretty nerve-wracking, I'll tell you, never knowing who was going to come through the kitchen door at any moment."

Edie brought her hands up to her mouth to stifle a laugh.

"I can just see that tub," she laughed. "All legs and arms sticking out of it."

"It was funny, all right," he said. "Especially the night my sister's girl friend caught me in the act of getting out of the tub."

"It must have been a great shock to her," Edie said, glancing mischievously at him.

"I don't know about her," he said, remembering the scene. "I know that it paralyzed me for a second or two, and we just stared at each other, then I tried to sit down too quickly and my seat hit the edge of the tub and the whole thing tipped over. She laughed then, and I sat with the tub pulled up in front of me and the water spilled all over the floor. I think I screamed at her, I don't remember, but I know she ran out, laughing."

"How old were you?" Tucker asked, laughing.

"Oh, it was during my senior year; I was seventeen and very shy and modest."

"How tall were you then?" Edie asked.

"Just about six-two. You know, I grew eleven inches during my junior and senior years. I remember that period as the tired years. It sure took a lot out of me, growing that fast. I really had an appetite. God, I was always eating."

"Did you play sports?" Tucker asked, remembering his own high-school days.

"Only basketball, and that for only one reason. You see, it was during the last years of the depression and I had to go out and earn some money to complement the family income."

"He worked in a cotton mill," Edie said, proudly. "Worked the three-to-twelve shift every day and brought home the same pay as any working man in his town. In the morning he would get up early and study before going to school. I think that was so marvelous of him," she said, quickly kissing Alan on the cheek.

"That's probably why he's a teacher today," Tucker said. "He had reasons to appreciate the importance of an education. How did you manage to get through college?"

"That came after the war. I went on the GI Bill."

"How do you like teaching?"

"It's the only thing I'd want to do," Alan said, leaning forward to look at Tucker. "It's something I can't explain. I don't think I could ever be satisfied doing anything else."

"That's the way I feel about being a cop," Tucker said, slightly embarrassed by the sudden intimacy in the conversation, but finding it important to tell Alan how he felt about his work.

"I can imagine," Alan said. "It's very important work."

"Yes, it's like teaching. It's important to have the right people doing the work. People who are qualified to do it right. People who are not just looking for a pay check every week, but people who feel a strong sense of dedication. People who realize that their jobs are more important than making automobiles or tooth paste. They must realize that theirs is a responsibility to the whole community. You can't do a job like this the way it should be done without dedication." Tucker stopped, then suddenly laughed. "Who wound me up," he said, glancing at Edie. "I'll bet you think I'm a nut."

"Oh, no," she said. "I would never think that."

"Hey, where are we?" Alan said, looking around. "This is Bel Air, isn't it?"

"Yeah," Tucker said. "I just thought you'd be interested in seeing Kahn's little castle in the hills."

"Smells wonderful," Edie said, taking a deep breath, her happy mood shattered by the mention of Kahn's name.

"There it is," Tucker said, slowing down the car as they stared at the huge sprawling building, now all lighted up, the driveway full of automobiles. The loud music floated out to them, and they would hear the rumble of laughing drifting through the music.

"I'd like to go home," Edie said, suddenly beginning to shiver, feeling the pain starting in back of her right eye. That was where the migraine always started, spreading quickly to the whole side of her head. Alan reached over and held her against him.

"Migraine?" he whispered.

"Yes."

"Home it is," Tucker said, and swung the car around and headed down the steep hill.

Al Rebos waited until he saw the car drive off with Alan and Edie before stepping out of the black sedan. He hurried up the stairs, the bulging briefcase tucked tightly under his arm.

Al's success had always depended on his discerning powers. His career was built on his ability to judge human nature. Usually, he would spend a long time studying the party in question. He would stake out and watch until he knew all the person's habits. Nothing was left to chance.

Rebos was engaged in a dangerous business and he had to be sure of the smallest detail before planting a bomb. There was no margin for error. A bomb going off and killing the wrong party could mean a lot of trouble. Al's career was flawless up to now, and he took a fastidious pride in this knowledge. Nothing should be allowed to mar such a fine record.

The Avery job was different. Here was a chance for error. It was a quick, pressure job; the kind that Al had always avoided. This was a job for some crazy punk, hungry for a fast buck; some junkhead needing a jolt. It was not a job for Al Rebos, the perfectionist.

All he had had was a quick look at the Averys. Quiet, dull couple. Wife pregnant. He had caught a quick glimpse of her when the door had opened. It was this quality that tempted him to take the chance; he was willing to bet his impeccable career that the Averys would be in bed when the bomb went off at one o'clock. In fact, he was sure they would be in bed by eleven—twelve at the very latest.

It was a safe margin. Worth the chance.

He placed the bomb in the storage compartment of the bed's headboard. He buried it under shorts, undershirts and socks, until the sharp ticking sound was softened and muffled beyond hearing.

Then he drove out to the airport, where he called Ricca, and took the ten o'clock flight back to Las Vegas.

19.

Little Abner had been in and out of the telephone booth at least twenty times in the last six hours. Each time he felt like calling Marty Kahn and telling him he couldn't do the job, and each time he chickened out as soon as he lifted the receiver off the hook.

There had been a lot of traffic in and out of Merkle's shop. It seemed as if every cop in the city had been in the place since Little Abner had staked out. Now there was only one cop left with Merkle, and Little Abner realized that it would probably have to be now or never.

Slowly, he oozed his huge body out of the phone booth and stared up and down the street. Merkle's shop was on the north side of the street, the second shop east of the street corner. All the streets running north and south in that area started at Sunset and ran downhill all the way south to Baldwin Hills, where they started going uphill again.

This geographical fact was the basis for the first original thought ever to strike Little Abner's skull. It was conceived in despair, nurtured in frustration, delivered in pain.

His face twisting in the effort of thought, he lumbered across Santa Monica Boulevard and hurried up Ashdale Street. He found the first car facing the intersection about thirty feet up the hill. Conveniently, the door was unlocked.

Little Abner opened the door and released the emergency brake, then quickly reached over and pulled the gear lever into neutral. The car started to roll down the hill and he ran beside it, steering and pushing, aiming it for the center of the intersection. The car gained speed and he stopped running, watching it roll down the street.

He waited a moment, then hopped clumsily around and plunged into the dark alley leading to the rear of Merkle's shop, hurrying in that peculiar lumbering gait of the uncoordinated, his big head rolling from side to side. The crash came just as he reached the rear window of the shop. He heard the wild screeching of brakes, followed by the agonized sound of twisting metal and breaking glass. Then he saw the uniformed policeman come running out of the partitioned room, with Merkle right behind him. Little Abner laughed hoarsely and slapped his thigh, his normally vacuous face a mixture of conflicting grimaces as he peered into the room, his nose flattened against the filthy window pane.

Then they were gone, disappearing down the sidewalk, and he rushed to the locked door and slammed his huge foot against it, the rotten wood bursting open under the tremendous pressure. He stood in the shattered doorway, filling it with his huge bulk, laughing, rubbing his hands gleefully together.

He looked around the room for some place to hide, some place where he could wait for Merkle, wait for the right moment. He walked into the room toward the front of the shop, to see if he could spot Merkle on the sidewalk. He had just reached the front counter when he heard the approaching footsteps outside. Quickly he scooted down on his hands and knees behind the counter.

First he saw the shoes, small and pointed and yellow. He looked up and saw the startled face of Merkle, and his big hands reached out and grabbed the thin legs.

Merkle screamed and tried to break away from the grip, but he was too late. Little Abner stood up, flipping Merkle upside down, holding him up by the ankles. Then, slowly, he raised up his arms, laughing into Merkle's terror-filled, incredulous eyes, staring up at him from a red, bulging face.

"No," he squeaked. "Lemme go."

Little Abner's arms came down and Merkle's head hit the floor with a dull thud. Then the arms came up again. Merkle's eyes were glazed with pain now and he held his bleeding head in his hands, the blood running through his fingers, dripping on the floor.

Little Abner laughed, choking and coughing, his huge body shaking convulsively.

"Airplane ride," he laughed, and spun around clumsily, whirling Merkle around, faster and faster, the speed straightening out Merkle's body horizontally.

"*Wheeeeee!*" Little Abner cried, the room beginning to spin crazily before his eyes, his body shaking with the hysterical laughter. "*Wheeee!*" he said, letting go one hand, searching for support as he almost stumbled and fell, still spinning, Merkle flying around like a pinwheel.

"Stop," the young uniformed policeman called from the doorway, the .38 Special in his hand aimed at Little Abner. "Put him down. Easy!"

Little Abner actually saw the policeman before he heard the words. He saw the gun and he tried to think. Then the words startled him and he let go of Merkle's ankle, let go right in the middle of the spin. Merkle flew, his arms and legs flapping as he sailed across the room and right through the plate-glass window.

Merkle knew it a split second before Little Abner released him. He felt a slackening of pressure around his ankle. Then he was airborne, and he felt the fear pounding hard all through his floating body. He screamed a loud, piercing, girlish shriek that violently tore at his throat. Then his head hit the plate glass, and he felt it buckle, and with it came the realization of death. He knew exactly what was happening now. And his mind calculated ahead, telling him what was happening before he felt the pain. The glass shattered as he flew through it. First his head, then his shoulders and arms, then his kicking feet. Everything at this moment was intense and horrifying as his body began to flip over as the speed of his flight diminished. He hit the sidewalk on the back of his head, his whole weight pressing down sharply, and he felt his neck snap, his mind feebly protesting against death. But death was upon him as he skidded across the sidewalk and over the curb.

Little Abner saw the gun come up and lurched sideways, bumping against the counter, his mind confused and dizzy from the spinning. The explosion thundered in the small room and Little Abner felt the sharp stab of pain in his stomach, knocking the wind out of him as he bent forward, his head twisting sideways, his hands gripping at the pain. The acrid smell of the gunpowder reached him then, and his confused mind became frantic.

Wildly he whirled and lunged toward the back door. Five more bullets hit him before he had taken five steps. He died there, his huge body stretched out in a pool of blood, his sluggish mind never understanding what had happened.

20.

Edie went to the bathroom for her injection while Alan put the water on to boil for the coffee. Tucker sat on the sofa, watching him.

"Won't be a minute," Alan said, looking up and smiling. "I hope you don't mind instant coffee."

"That'll be fine," Tucker said, getting up and walking up to him. "Look," he said. "I hope you don't take this wrong, but I brought a gun for you. Just in case. You know what I mean?"

"I'm not sure I do," Alan said.

"I'm gonna be in charge of the detail assigned to protect you. We're gonna do the best we can, but you never can tell. Now, don't get me wrong. I'm not trying to scare you. In fact, that's the last thing I want to do. All I want is for you to be careful, and also, prepared. I've got a shotgun in the car. Okay?"

"I don't need it. I've got a rifle."

"What kind?"

"A thirty-thirty Winchester."

"No good for this kind of thing. Take my word for it. The shotgun will be a lot better. I'll go down and get it for you."

"No. Wait. I don't want Edie to know about it. It will just worry her."

"Okay, come down and get it after she goes to bed."

"It might be quite a wait for you."

"Forget it. I plan to spend a little time around here tonight anyway."

"There's no need for that. They gave me twenty-four hours."

"Don't worry about it. I don't have anything else to do. You come down after she goes to bed. Okay?"

"All right. I appreciate your concern, but I really don't think it's necessary."

"Look, you let us professionals worry about whether it's necessary or not. That's what we're paid for."

"Well," Alan grinned. "If that's the case, I submit without another word. I certainly wouldn't want to encroach on your territory."

"What's that?" Edie asked, coming out of the bathroom,

smiling.

"Feeling better, I see," Tucker said.

"Much."

"Wonderful," Alan said, pouring the boiling water into the cups.

"Would you like something to eat?" Edie asked, smiling at the two men.

"Not for me," Tucker said. "Coffee is just fine."

"Nor me," Alan said. "But how about junior?"

"Never mind junior," she said. "He's big enough now."

"Gonna be a boy, heh?" Tucker said.

"Of course," Alan said. "That's what I asked for."

"Oh," Tucker said. "That's fine."

"Idiots," Edie laughed. "It's going to be twin girls."

"There," Alan said, as they all sat down at the dining table. "That settles it."

"I enjoyed the ride," Edie said, smiling at Tucker. "It was very nice of you to take us. We appreciate it."

"Don't mention it," Tucker said. "My pleasure."

"Are you here for any particular reason?" she asked, casually spooning sugar into her coffee.

Tucker looked quickly at Alan before answering. "Well," he said, "in a way I am. You know we just can't ignore that threat. It's our job to give you all the protection you need."

"Thank you," Edie said. "It's very kind of you."

"Well!" Tucker stammered, feeling that he had to be honest with such a straight-forward woman. "It's not ex-actly kindness. You see your husband is a very valuable witness. We need him very much to make our case stick. That's the real reason we're protecting you."

"I appreciate your honesty," she said, standing up, forc-ing her facial muscles into a smile. "Now, if you'll excuse me, I think I'll go to bed. Good night, Sergeant Tucker." She held her hand out to him and he stood up and shook it gently, yet firmly.

"All right, dear," Alan said, standing up. "I'll be in pretty soon."

She came forward and kissed Alan on the lips, softly, gently, her warm lips lingering for just a second.

It was eleven o'clock when Edie Avery slipped into bed.

By eleven o'clock the party at Marty Kahn's place was really jumping. Busty, creamy, heavy-lidded starlets jiggled about in low-cut, skin-tight sheaths. Writers, actors and hoodlums mingled in little groups, and drank and smoked and talked and laughed, their arms casually draped around firm, opulent bodies, patting rounded little butts, brushing against pointed breasts. Jazz blared out of hidden speakers, filling the room with its driving beat. There was the clicking of glasses, the loud guffaw, the low, sensuous laugh, the high-pitched nervous giggle.

Marty Kahn stood in the center of the room, his pudgy face red and excited, his arms waving as he talked to a young writer from one of the national magazines.

"I'm giving it to you straight," he said. "I've never been knocked out. I've lost a couple of T.K.O.'s, but never a knockout."

"How many fights did you have?"

"Christ, who keeps count. I fought them all. I was the hardest-hitting welter in the business, but I didn't have no goddam reach. See," he raised his arms, "too goddam short."

"Well, look, Mr. Kahn, my magazine might be interested in doing a factual piece on you. Nothing sensational, but we would want all the facts."

"That's what I'm giving you. Why don't you take notes?"

"Not now. First I'd just like to talk to you. Get the feel of it. Then we can sit down, maybe next week, and work it out."

"What kind of facts are you interested in?"

"Well—" he gave a nervous laugh—"the stuff that hasn't been told before. Your childhood, schooling, fighting career, that type of thing."

"Yeah. How about this layout?"

"That too, of course, but later. We might do a series if we can get enough pertinent material."

"Well, there's plenty of that. Don't you worry."

"Fine."

"What's the circulation of your rag?"

"About six million. Goes all over the world."

"Yeah. How about pictures for this piece?"

"It will be illustrated."

"Color?"

"Some. It all depends on you, Mr. Kahn. If we get some good exclusive information, you know, something powerful enough to make an exciting article, then we'll really do it up brown."

"Yeah," Marty said, grinning. "Well, I'll fix you up. Don't worry."

Cliff Spar, the foremost celebrity at the party stood behind the sofa, leaning over Marie, offering her a drink from his glass. He had an unobstructed view down the front of her gown and as she reached over for the glass he saw clearly that she was not wearing a brassiere. He leaned down further and whispered into her ear.

"Tonight is the night," he said, letting his lips brush against her ear.

Marie glanced up coyly from under heavy eyelashes. "The night for what?" she asked.

"You know," he whispered again, his lips sliding down to her earlobe. "Tonight is gonna be your opening night." Then the earlobe was in his mouth and he bit it gently.

Marie didn't move as cold shivers tingled down her spine, making gooseflesh on her arms and legs. "You're silly," she said.

"It's gonna be the biggest night of the year," he whispered. "If you know what I mean." And he let his hand drop on her shoulder, his fingers gently, secretly pulling at the shoulder strap for a better view down the front of her dress. "Those look pretty good. Real juicy."

She giggled and quickly looked around the room for Marty. He was still in the center of the room, talking to that writer who was so good-looking, but not as good-looking as Cliff Spar. She turned back and gave Spar a long, seductive look. Then she raised his glass to her lips and emptied it.

"Sit down," she said. "I'll get you a refill."

"Don't be long," he said, and leaped over the sofa, landing in a sitting position.

He waited for her, his mind busy trying to figure a way of getting her alone. There had to be someplace in this goddam house.

He saw her coming, her wide hips undulating, the tight dress rippling over her flat stomach, her large breasts straining against the thin material. He let his right hand drop on the sofa, just idly lying there, and he smiled up at her as she sat down on his hand. She jumped, startled, spilling some of the drink, but he pushed her back down again, all the time smiling, his eyes slightly glazed and fixed by the wild surging urgency that stirred through him.

He felt her warm, soft buttocks pressing down on his hand, and he moved it slightly until it was centered. His voice was low and husky when he spoke.

"I've never wanted anyone more than I want you right now," he whispered, his face moving close to hers. "I want you so much I ache."

"Don't," she said, her face flushed, her eyes narrowed by the heavy lids. "Don't move your hand." And she shifted her weight slightly. "Kiss me," she whispered, closing her eyes.

He moved back, startled by the request. "Not here," he whispered hoarsely. "Let's go somewhere."

"Where?"

"I don't know."

"Wait. I know." She opened her eyes and he saw the wild desire in them. "The den. I'll get the key. Meet me in there in five minutes."

Evangelist Willy Brand was a tall, ascetic-looking man with thick curly hair and a low forehead. Willy Brand had the kind of voice that swayed people, and it swayed no one more than it did Willy Brand. Once he started talking, the sound of it intoxicated him, and he talked on and on, moved by the sound and the fury and the rhythm. He never really knew what he was saying. That he left up to God.

Willy Brand had a large following of fanatic believers, and he performed the most extraordinary miracles without the slightest effort. In fact, he performed dozens of miracles on television every Sunday night.

Willy's first ambition had been to be a movie star. He came to Hollywood during the Second World War, when there was a shortage of actors, and he did bit parts for six years. It took him that long to lose his Georgia accent. After that he drifted from job to job until that eventful night he attended an old-fashioned revival meeting and got religion. From then on he was a man of God, doing the Lord's work, bringing salvation to poor sinners.

Willy had three important assets. He had a loud, monotonous voice; he was a good ham; and he looked virile as all hell. Unlike his acting career, Willy's preaching career skyrocketed him to fame and fortune overnight.

Willy's greatest appeal was to women. He was to religion

what Elvis Presley was to rock 'n' roll. Middle-aged women moaned and screamed when Willy got to preaching. He stood on the stage, waving his arms, shaking his bony frame with an occasional wiggle of the hips, tearing his tie and jacket off, his face pale and ascetic under the low, Neanderthal forehead.

Willy's latest mission was to bring religion to Marty Kahn. He had heard and read a lot about Kahn, and every bit of information had intrigued him. Marty Kahn was the kind of man Willy Brand secretly admired.

He sat now in a fat upholstered chair, watching the spectacle unfolding before him. He puffed on a long, black cigar and smiled knowingly when Marie stood up and left the room. Five minutes later, Cliff Spar got up and looked around, then casually strolled out. Willy slapped his knee and laughed, his eyes turning to Marty, who still stood in the center of the room, talking to the young writer, unaware of Marie's disappearance.

The voice startled him out of his thoughts.

"I know you," said a pink-haired, pale-faced, green-eyed goddess in a gold lamé dress of obvious design. "You're that famous preacher, ain't you?"

"Bless your little heart," he said, jumping to his feet. "You startled me."

"Oh, gee," she said, trying to look hurt. "I'm sorry."

"No, no," he said. "I'm honored by the attention of such a divine little creature. What is your little name?"

"I'm Niki," she cooed.

"Bless you, child, that's a glorious little name. Simply heaven-inspired. That's what it is," he said, striking his most virile pose. "Inspired by the angels in heaven."

"Oh, you," she giggled. "You're making fun of me."

"I'm a big tease," he said, placing his hand on her shoulder. "Please sit down."

"Here," she said, pushing him back into the chair. "I'll

sit on the arm. See, just like this." And she sat down, smiling at him coyly through heavy mascaraed eyes, her swelling breasts directly in front of his eyes.

"Well, now, that's mighty nice," he said, giving her his most powerful soul-saving smile.

"You're cute," she said, and giggled nervously, shifting slightly on the arm of the chair, her breast briefly rubbing against his nose.

"Well, thank you," he said, trying to ignore the flippant breast. "Are you with the Lord, my child—" and he patted her knee spiritually. "Have you found your peace?"

"Oh, you," she giggled, and leaned her elbow against the back of the chair.

He laughed and looked up, his eyes barely inches away from her close-shaven armpit, and he saw the dark roots, the even texture of the flesh. It was like looking through a magnifying glass. It suddenly became the most desirable thing he had ever seen. It was flesh. It was hair. It was sex in its most basic form. He glanced up and looked into the green, teasing, knowing eyes. He knew that the vein down the center of his forehead was swollen and thumping furiously.

"You like me?" she asked, forming the words carefully.

"Yes, little one. I'm gonna help you find your way to God."

"I'm serious," she said, without smiling, her eyes covered by the heavy lids again. He patted her knee a couple of times, then slowly his fingers closed over the firm, nyloned leg and he squeezed, bringing his face up close, and she moved forward, her breast pressing against his cheek.

"Take me home," she murmured.

"Good Lord," he said, his voice hoarse and shaking, his face paralyzed against the warm, soft breast.

"Forget the Lord," she whispered without moving. "Think of me."

The vein dividing his low forehead was dark and throbbing. He squeezed the knee a little more and his hand slipped up her leg a fraction. "Praise the Lord," he said. "While we banish Satan."

"You're crazy," she said, moving away, looking down at him, annoyed.

"I do the work of the Lord," he said, and moved closer, trying to re-establish contact with the breast. "We must ask the Lord for strength. We are but poor, miserable sinners. Weak of flesh and spirit. Pray with me, my dear. Pray for salvation."

Niki laughed and stood up. "Man, you're gone," she said. "Real gone." And she hurried away, leaving him sitting there with nothing but the throbbing vein.

The frustration sent anger flowing through his now limp body. Dark, seething anger that grew into a wild fury. He glared across the room, seeking a target for his monstrous hate, and saw Marty Kahn talking to Joe Ricca. Suddenly he was on his feet and striding across the room to the side of the two men.

"I'm leaving this house of sin and shame," he shouted, his face red and bulging.

"What's wrong with you?" Kahn demanded.

"The wrong is not with me," he cried. "It is with you and yours. See for yourself. Go find your mistress in the arms of another. Run to your den. Hurry. Find their perspiring limbs locked together in sinful embrace." And he spun around and ran out of the house....

Cliff Spar buckled his belt and moved away from the leather sofa and the reclining Marie.

"Put your dress on," he said, lighting a cigarette.

She lay on the white sofa, her gold-brown body still quivering with hunger. "Again," she said, holding her arms out to him. "Again."

"Later," he said.

"No, now, this minute."

"What do you think I am?" He laughed nervously.

"I know what you are," she said, wantonly pressing her hands against her body, looking at him through narrowed lids, her lips parted. "You started something. Now finish it."

"Have a heart," he said.

"Come here," she said, "and I'll give you one."

"For God's sake, what's wrong with you?"

"You started it," she shouted, suddenly up on her elbows, her eyes wide with hate. "Be a man and finish it."

"I need a drink," he said, going to the bar.

"You dirty son of a bitch," she screamed, jumping off the sofa.

"Good God!" he cried, backing away from the bar, his mouth sagging open, his eyes wide and unbelieving. "God almighty, what is that?" He pointed at the curled up body of Bryce Barker lying behind the bar.

Marie ran forward and stopped, stunned by the sight. Slowly she dropped to her knees before the now cold, stiff body and stared at the waxen features, the glazed, sightless eyes.

Then she cried, the sobs shaking her body, her hands pressed into her mouth, her eyes stricken with pain and terror. Bryce Barker, the only man who had ever shown any respect for her, lying dead, tied up like a little ball. And there was more, too, more than just regret for a nice guy. There was the feeling of secret passion. She remembered the nights she had dreamed of Barker, and how in her mind she had fashioned a great romance.

She threw herself on him, pressing her nude body against the stiff, cold flesh.

She kissed him hungrily. She cried hysterically, rocking and moaning on her bended knees.

The door flew open and Marty ran into the room. Ricca closed the door and leaned against it, smiling.

Marty saw Marie, nude, on her knees before Barker's body, and struck out with his foot.

She felt the foot smash into her side and the wind flew out of her lungs. She looked up, stunned, gasping for breath. He kicked again, this time the foot striking the base of her spine. She cried out in pain, rolling on the floor, her hands clutching her back. The foot swung out again and caught her in the neck, just behind the ear. Lights exploded in her head and she lost consciousness.

"You dirty, filthy bitch," Marty screamed, standing over her. Then he looked up and saw Cliff Spar, staring at him, his ashen face slack with fear.

"You son of a bitch. You lousy whoremaster," Marty shouted, leaping towards him.

"Don't," Spar cried, his hands covering his million-dollar face. "Please, Marty. We're friends."

Marty lashed out with his hard fists, working quickly, viciously, the years of boxing skill making him look like a machine. Spar's nose was the first thing to go. He screamed, his eyes unbelieving, his hands covering the smashed bone. Then Marty drove half a dozen solid jolts into his stomach, and Spar forgot the nose, and Marty went back to work on the face, drawing blood with every sharp, vicious swipe of his knuckles. Spar crumbled to the floor, whimpering, begging for mercy. Marty struck out with his foot then and slowly and methodically muti-lated the huddled body.

"Take it easy," Ricca called out, the smile still on his lips. "You'll kill the bastard."

Marty stopped and looked back at Ricca. "Get him out of here," he said. "But first clear out the place. The party is over."

"How about the alibi?" Ricca said, looking at this watch.

"It's only midnight. The bomb's not set to go for another hour."

"Screw the alibi. Get them out of here. Go on!"

Ricca left and Marty looked around the room, first at Spar, then at Marie, and finally at Barker. Slowly, he approached the rolled-up body, knowing he was dead the moment he saw him. He stood above him and looked down and the anger evaporated. There was only pity and sadness left. The empty, gnawing feeling was there again in the pit of his stomach.

Manic Marty Kahn was going into another depression.

21.

Alan Avery went into the bedroom and stood by the bed looking down at Edie. She lay on her right side, her knees curled up, her breathing steady and even. He leaned over and kissed her forehead very gently, then went back into the living room.

He didn't feel like sleeping; he had too much on his mind. He glanced across the room at the two guns leaning against the closet door, the 12-gauge double-barreled shotgun and the .30-30 Winchester rifle. Both were loaded.

He didn't really know why he had loaded them. He knew he could never use them; even if his home were violated, he couldn't imagine himself using them.

He went into the kitchen for a drink of water, then went back into the living room and sat down. He reached over to the bookshelves behind the chair and pulled out Whitman's *Leaves of Grass*.

He opened it and let the pages flick slowly by his thumb, the magical phrases jumping up at him from the printed pages:

> *Come, I will make the continent indissoluble*
> *I will make divine magnetic lands,*
> > *with the love of comrades*

> *My tongue, every atom of my blood, form'd*
> > *from this soil, this air ...*
> *Have you reckon'd a thousand acres much?*
> > *have you reckon'd the earth much?*

> *Out of the cradle endlessly rocking,*

> *When lilacs last in the dooryard bloom'd*

He stopped a moment, his finger frozen on the page, his eyes staring at the words, unseeing, as his mind floated away into the past and he saw the green rolling hills of New Hampshire and he remembered the warm Sunday afternoons he had spent lying in the tall grass, reading the wonderful poems of Whitman. He remembered how they had filled him so full of love for the whole world that he could hardly contain himself. He had felt as if he were going to burst inside. He remembered one verse in particular and he thumbed through the book now, looking for it, suddenly becoming very important to him.

He found it and read it slowly, getting the same old thrill:

> *I believe a leaf of grass is no less*
> > *than the journeywork of the stars,*
> *And the pismire is equally perfect, and a grain*
> > *of sand, and the egg of the wren,*
> *And the tree-toad is a chef-d'oeuvre*
> *for the highest,*
> *And the running blackberry would adorn*
> > *the parlors of heaven,*

*And the narrowest hinge is my hand
    puts to scorn all machinery,
And the cow crunching with depress'd head
    surpasses any statue,
And a mouse is miracle enough to stagger
    sextillions of infidels …*

He stopped and brushed the tears that threatened to spill down his cheeks. He felt in one of those moods when words, the right words, really moved him. Whitman could always do it; he held the string to his heart. And at times like now, when everything was wrong, he couldn't find a better prophet to consult. He glanced down the page, stopping at the next verse:

*I think I could turn and live with animals,
    they're so placid and self-contain'd,
I stand and look at them long and long.
They do not sweat and whine about their condition,
They do not lie awake in the dark and weep
    for their sins,
They do not make me sick discussing their duty to
God,
Not one is dissatisfied, not one is demented
    with the mania of owning things,
No one kneels to another, nor to his kind
    that lived thousands of years ago,
Not one is respectable or industrious over
    the whole earth.*

He closed the book and closed his eyes. Why did there have to be violence and cruelty in the world? That was the only thing he really hated; he could take everything else, stupidity, ignorance, laziness, all of it. But not the meanness and viciousness of the cruel ones, the violent ones, the greedy ones like Ricca and Kahn, men without hearts, without feelings, without sensitivity, without souls. Men hungry for power. Men willing to inflict pain and suffering to achieve their objective.

He thought of Edie and her fears. And he remembered what he had told her about his own fears: that he was not trying to be a hero, it simply was a question of principles. Anything else would be physically, mentally and spiritually impossible. It couldn't be reckoned on a basis of life and death. It was too deep, too ingrained, too much a way of life. Nothing could change it, not even the fear of death.

The dynamite bomb went off, as set, at one o'clock.

The bedroom wall burst open and Alan flew out of his chair. He lay on the floor, shocked and dazed, as the whole house rocked and shook in the deafening blast. Then he was coughing, trying to breathe in the smoky, dust-filled room, crawling toward the shattered bedroom wall, all motions arrested and fuzzy, everything weird and unreal.

There was glass and plaster all over the floor and he felt it dig and cut into the palms of his hands and into his knees. And with this awareness came the full realization of what had happened, and he rose to his feet, screaming, his heart pounding with terror as he raced into the bedroom.

The bed was a brilliant inferno. He ran to it, feeling the flames lick at his face and clothes, and he moved back to stamp out the fire starting on his shirt sleeve, and he saw in the nightmarish light of the flames the torn, mutilated, flaming body of Edie, and he threw himself into the flames, screaming, pulling at the flaming corpse, unaware of the fire licking at his clothes and flesh.

Then Tucker was tugging at Alan, pulling him out of the burning bedroom, ripping Alan's flaming shirt off, using all his strength to hold him back.

Something snapped in Alan's mind. The shock was too

great to accept. He lashed out at Tucker, striking hard with his fists, then quickly reached down and grabbed a broken piece of studding and struck Tucker across the top of the head. Tucker fell to his knees and Alan struck again. Tucker sank to the floor, unconscious.

Alan ran back into the bedroom and stopped before the now smoldering bed and the shrunken, twisted, cremated body that had once been the sweet, talking, walking, loving Edie. And he screamed and pulled his hair, and ran out of the room, blinded by the tears, bumping and tripping over the rubble,

Then he had the guns, the rifle and shotgun, in his arms and was running down the stairs to the street and Tucker's car.

Hate.

A blind, surging hate was all he felt. And it was like the vilest poison racing through his veins, pounding to every part of his body, shrieking for revenge. For the kill.

Ricca and Kahn would have to die. Alan knew that as he drove recklessly toward Bel Air. The crying had turned to sobs now. Great, choking sobs that shook his thin frame with the violence of a storm.

Anger and hate, the emotions of violence, were a part of him as he drove in the night, leaving death behind, crying for what could never again be: a smiling, dancing, loving Edie.

Sweet Edie.

The speeding car skidded around a sharp curve and continued its steep climb up the Bel Air road.

The party was over.

Marty Kahn was in the bedroom, pacing before the big bed, glaring at Marie. She lay in the bed, the covers pulled up to her face, her eyes hard as stone.

"I'm throwing you out on your ass," he said, fighting

the gnawing emptiness that was quickly spreading upward, until he could feel it pressing under his heart.

He couldn't get rid of the image of Barker's body tied up in a little ball, his waxen face and sightless eyes. He had always liked Barker, always enjoyed talking to him, especially when Barker was in one of his talking moods. Kahn had learned a lot from Barker. Learned a lot about things like history and books and science, particularly, astronomy. Barker had always liked talking about the stars and the planets. Sometimes he would talk about things that Kahn could not understand, like the time he had compared the universe to an atom, and had jokingly said that maybe we were just an electron in some atom in somebody's chair. Something like that. Kahn couldn't remember too well. Anyway, it was too deep for him. But it had been interesting and exciting. Barker's eyes had lighted up and his face had been full of enthusiasm as he had talked, developing the idea as he went along, actually thinking out loud.

Kahn shrugged his shoulders. Well, so what? He had asked for it, getting wise like that. Who the hell did he think he was anyway. Nobody got wise with Marty Kahn. Nobody!

"And to think," he shouted, getting back to Marie, "I almost married you. You filthy bitch. Well, you're all done around here. I want you out of here first thing in the morning. Understand?"

Marie stared at him without answering. She also was thinking of Bryce Barker, remembering how nice he had always been to her, never leering like the others because she was Marty's mistress. Bryce had been sophisticated. He had understood life. He had smiled at her, openly, frankly; and often, she was sure, admiringly. He had treated her as an equal. Told her funny stories. Some clean, some shady, some downright filthy. She had laughed at all of them. And with the laughter had come a bond. A silent relationship that she never quite understood, except that she often thought about Bryce. Dreamed about him. Imagined herself in his arms. And Marie being Marie, she also imagined herself in bed with him, making soft, delicate love together. She always woke from those dreams with a warm feeling in her groin.

"Understand!" Marty shouted again, running to the bed and shaking his fist before her eyes.

And she turned over in the bed, away from the fist, still without answering.

"God damn it," he growled. "I'm talking to you." And he grabbed a handful of hair and twisted her head around to face him. "I'd just as soon put a bullet through you as look at you," he said. "You filthy bitch!"

Suddenly, she sat up in the bed and waved her small fist at him, her whole body shaking with anger.

"And what are you?" she cried. "What gives you the right to call me names?"

"Shut up," he shouted, the depression black and vicious in him.

"Murderer!" she cried.

"Shut up," he shouted, and swung his open hand against her cheek, the sound cracking in the room.

"You killed Bryce," she cried, covering her cheek with her hand. "He was ten times the man you'll ever be. And you killed him. Murderer! Dirty, lousy murderer!"

His fist caught her on the side of the head just slightly in front of the temple and she fell back on the bed, stifling the cry that rose in her throat. She waited without flinching for the other blows to fall, but nothing happened.

Then she heard the loud clang of the warning signal. Someone had penetrated the electric eye. She looked up and saw Marty running out of the room.

Alan was doing sixty when he reached the entrance to Kahn's home. He twisted the wheel sharply and drove the car right through the tall wrought-iron gate. There was a loud, crashing sound and the steering wheel jerked crazily out of his hands, but the car kept going, knocking the gate to one side, rolling up toward the front of the house.

Alan jumped out of the car and ran up to the front door like a marine storming a beachhead, gripping the guns at his side. The door was locked.

He pulled the trigger to the shotgun and it jumped in his hand as the door burst open, slamming against the wall.

He saw three men standing in the center of the living room, staring at him, their mouths open in astonishment, and in that split second before he pulled the trigger, he recognized all of them. Ricca and Doto from the line-up and Marty Kahn from the many pictures in the newspapers.

The shotgun exploded and he saw Doto fall, his face covered with blood. Then he dropped the shotgun and the rifle began jerking and jumping in his hand and the slugs were smashing all over the room.

Ricca ran forward, his hands before his face, and Alan steadied the gun in his two hands and aimed.

The slug caught him just under the chin, going through his hand first, then coming out the top of his head. He fell sideways, first on one knee, then over on his back.

Alan saw Marty turn and run and he touched the trigger again, and saw Marty stop and spin around, his arms extended, his face pleading; then he fell flat on his stomach.

Alan stood in the center of the room, his breathing impaired, trying to catch his breath, the room blurred and whirling. He dropped the gun and started for the open door.

Something exploded in his chest.

He staggered a few steps and felt his legs crumble under him.

It was much worse than the first time in the parking lot. It was bigger and hotter and stronger. It was as if his heart had burst apart, flying into tiny pieces.

He fell, his hands grasping at his throat, trying to take in air, his heart jerking in his chest, rapping against his ribs.

He waited for death, not struggling anymore, accepting death calmly. And he thought of Edie, trying to see her in his mind, but all he saw was the twisted, darkened remains on the bed, and he cried out against the pain the image evoked.

This was a nightmare. It had to be. These things did not and could not happen to a quiet, law-abiding schoolteacher. And he wondered about life and dreams, and which was which. This could not be reality. It did not feel like reality. Nothing about it felt real, not even the pain in his chest.

He tried to sit up, propping himself on his elbows, hoping he would wake up in the warm bed at Edie's side, and the pain in his chest exploded again, this time sending a warm searing pain across his whole chest, and he tried to breathe, his mouth reaching up for air, his face turning blue, his eyes rolling in his head.

Then he fell back to the floor....

Tucker found him like that when he arrived five minutes later. He leaned over Alan, his ear against his chest, listening for a heartbeat. He reached over and pressed the eyelids closed over the sightless eyes, then he stood up and looked over the room.

Ricca and Doto lay dead where they had dropped.

Marty Kahn lay on his stomach, his face pressed against the thick, luxurious carpet, his big eyes open and full of pain.

"Help me," he murmured. "Please."

Tucker picked up the Winchester and walked up to Marty and looked down at him.

Slowly, carefully, he placed the muzzle of the rifle against Marty's head and pulled the trigger. The gun made a muffled, swishing sound against the head.

Tucker put down the gun and walked across the room to the telephone. He picked up the receiver and started to dial headquarters.

He looked up and saw Marie. She was standing at the end of the hallway, watching him. She came forward, slowly at first, then more quickly, until she was running. She went by Tucker and stopped before Marty. She looked down at the bloody head, and, leaning over quickly, she spat on it. Then she ran back up the hall and disappeared into her room.

Tucker watched her go, then completed his call.

THE END

OVID DEMARIS BIBLIOGRAPHY
(1919-1998)

NOVELS

The Slasher (1956)

The Hoods Take Over (1957; filmed as Gang War, 1958)

Ride the Gold Mare (1957)

The Lusting Drive (1958)

The Long Night (1959)

The Enforcer (1960)

The Extortioners (1960)

The Gold-Plated Sewer (1960)

Chips' Girls (1961, as by Oscar J. Demaris; reprinted in UK as Mason's Women, 1971)

Candyleg (1961; filmed as Machine Gun McCain, 1969, reprinted as such, 1970)

The Parasite (1963)

The Organization (1964; reprinted as The Fatal Mistake, 1966; and The Contract, 1970)

The Overlord (1972)

The Vegas Legacy (1983)

Ricochet (1988)

NON-FICTION

"Lucky" Luciano (1960; reprinted as The Lucky Luciano Story, 1969)

The Dillinger Story (1961; reprinted as Dillinger, 1973)

The Lindbergh Kidnaping Case (1961)

The Green Felt Jungle (w/Ed Reid; 1963)

America the Violent (1970)

Captive City: Chicago in Chains (1970)

Poso del Mundo: Inside the Mexican-American Border from Tijuana to Matamoros (1970)

Dirty Business: The Corporate-Political Money-Power Game (1974)

The Director: An Oral Biography of J. Edgar Hoover
  (1975)
Brothers in Blood: The International Terrorist Network
  (1977)
Judith Exner: My Story (as told to Ovid Demaris; 1978)
The Last Mafioso: The Treacherous World of Jimmy
  Frantianno (1980)
Boardwalk Jungle (1986)
Jack Ruby: The Man Who Killed the Man Who Killed
  Kennedy (w/Garry Wills; 1994)
J. Edgar Hoover: As They Knew Him (1994)

Ovid Demaris (given name Ovide E. Desmarais) was born September 6, 1919 in Biddeford, Maine. After serving in the U.S. Army Air Forces, he graduated from College of Idaho in 1948 and Boston University in 1950. He then became a United Press correspondent and newspaper  reporter, before turning to writing books, both fiction and non-fiction, most of them featuring organized crime. Demaris is best known as the co-author of *The Green Felt Jungle*, an expose of the Mafia in Las Vegas, and *The Last Mafioso*, his biography of Jimmy Fratianno. Two of his novels were turned into films, including *The Hoods Take Over*. Demaris passed away on March 12, 1998, also in Biddeford, Maine.

Black Gat Books

Black Gat Books is a new line of pocket paperbacks introduced in 2015 by Stark House Press. New titles appear every three months, featuring the best in crime fiction reprints. Each book is sized to 4.25" x 7", just like they used to be. Collect them all!

1 Haven for the Damned
by Harry Whittington
978-1-933586-75-5, $9.99

2 Eddie's World
by Charlie Stella
978-1-933586-76-2, $9.99

3 Stranger at Home
by Leigh Brackett writing as
George Sanders
978-1-933586-78-6, $9.99

4 The Persian Cat
by John Flagg
978-1933586-90-8, $9.99

5 Only the Wicked
by Gary Phillips
978-1-933586-93-9, $9.99

6 Felony Tank
by Malcolm Braly
978-1-933586-91-5, $9.99

7 The Girl on the Bestseller List
by Vin Packer
978-1-933586-98-4, $9.99

8 She Got What She Wanted
by Orrie Hitt
978-1-944520-04-5, $9.99

9 The Woman on the Roof
by Helen Nielsen
978-1-944520-13-7, $9.99

10 Angel's Flight
by Lou Cameron
978-1-944520-18-2, $9.99

11 The Affair of Lady Westcott's
Lost Ruby / The Case of the
Unseen Assassin by Gary Lovisi
978-1-944520-22-9, $9.99

12 The Last Notch
by Arnold Hano
978-1-944520-31-1, $9.99

13 Never Say No to a Killer
by Clifton Adams
978-1-944520-36-6, $9.99

14 The Men from the Boys
by Ed Lacy
978-1-944520-46-5, $9.99

15 Frenzy of Evil
by Henry Kane
978-1-944520-53-3, $9.99

16 You'll Get Yours
by William Ard
978-1-944520-54-0, $9.99

17 End of the Line
by Dolores & Bert Hitchens
978-1-944520-57-1, $9.99

18 Frantic
by Noël Calef
978-1-944520-66-3, $9.99

Stark House Press

1315 H Street, Eureka, CA 95501   707-498-3135
griffinskye3@sbcglobal.net   www.starkhousepress.com

Available from your local bookstore or direct from the publisher.